GRILLOS

ONE MAN'S MISSION TO EXPOSE THE CORRUPT LINK BETWEEN
THE DRUGS TRADE AND THE HIGHEST LEVELS OF GOVERNMENT

H J VAN DE KOPPEL

GRILLOS

ONE MAN'S MISSION TO EXPOSE THE CORRUPT LINK BETWEEN
THE DRUGS TRADE AND THE HIGHEST LEVELS OF GOVERNMENT

MEMOIRS

Cirencester

Published by Memoirs

MEMOIRS

Memoirs Books

25 Market Place, Cirencester, Gloucestershire, GL7 2NX

info@memoirsbooks.co.uk   www.memoirsbooks.co.uk

Copyright © H J van de Koppel, October 2011

First published in England, October 2011

Book jacket design Ray Lipscombe

ISBN 978-1-908223-30-2

Printed in England

Dedication

For Leendert, one of the biggest originals one can meet – a privilege to have had your support while writing and always your friendship in life.

For Carlota, my "manager" who from the very beginning always supported me. This project has come about only thanks to your dedication and persistence.

Foreword

The drugs business has now been with us as an industry for over 40 years.

It is an industry which in 2009 'served' more than 210 million people globally, according to the United Nations Office on Drugs & Crime.

Think of the volume it has produced, and will keep on producing. Worldwide.

The drugs business moves, directly and indirectly, incalculable amounts of money. Billions.

It is estimated that between the border areas of Mexico and the USA alone more than US$40 billion worth is moved every year.

The drugs business is directly and indirectly connected to one of the highest mortality rates. We'll never know the exact figures.

There are people who made their fortunes in the drugs business and got out. Should we care?

Yes – because the recycled billions have re-entered the system. Our system.

And they will continue to do so.

CONTENTS

GRILLOS

New Jersey's Green Fields Cemetery, 1996

Why did people feel the need to put on such serious faces when they went to the funeral of someone like Lenny Gerstner – a man who had always made people laugh?

Paul Anfield wasn't listening to the speech by the senior partner of Lewman, Applebaum and Fromm, one of New York's most prestigious and blue-blooded law firms. It wasn't for him, even though Uncle Lenny had been his mentor and uncle; it was Lenny who had made him realise that life after studying business and administration law should be fun, as well as hard work.

The senior partner's voice droned on. 'Lenny's view and perception of people in business and business people was outstanding, and has led our firm as a guiding light...'

Paul's uncle had passed away as a result of a heart attack, which had not been unexpected; Lenny had had a heart condition, brought on by his lifestyle. He had lived the life of all the old New Yorkers from his profession - dry Martini lunches, two or three Cuban cigars a day, entertaining every night. After more than 40 years in business, Lenny had a wonderful soul in an abused body.

Yet his uncle had relished the abuse. This was a people business, and if you didn't like that side of professional life you shouldn't be a top corporate lawyer.

At least, plenty of people had shown up on this rainy Monday in February at the Green Fields Cemetery, 10 miles south of New Jersey. Uncle Lenny always liked to have people around, and after all this was his last public appearance.

As Paul looked around at the faces of his family, he registered again the three foreign faces he had seen earlier. They had to be Latin. Where did they fit in? Not family, that was for sure.

The two men were small and compact. The smooth way they were moving about didn't fit in with the way people behaved at funerals. But it was the woman who attracted immediate attention. She was tall, in a bright red designer suit, and she had a beautiful tanned face, the kind only darker-skinned women have. Her face didn't have a trace of make-up. Nor did it show any emotion, but she didn't look bored either. She seemed to be concentrating on something else entirely. Whatever it was, she was a stunner. She would have been beautiful in any place, at any time, in any circumstances.

And she resembled someone, Paul felt. Someone glamorous from the movies. Someone he had seen in a film from the seventies, perhaps? He just couldn't place her.

With difficulty he tried to turn his attention back to the eulogy.

'Lenny Gerstner's example to the legal profession was and will be based on human principals, trust and....' the Senior Partner droned on. He was interrupted by the bark of a dog – Prodeo, Uncle Lenny's fat black Labrador, who had been his most trusted companion since the death of his wife Doris more than 10 years before. Prodeo kept right on barking. He didn't stop until someone had put him into a car.

This interruption brought the Senior Partner's speech to an end sooner than he had probably imagined, giving another member of the family just enough opportunity to say the customary Thank-You-All-For-Being-Here-The-Family-Will-Remember-You-All-In-Their-Prayers. The coffin was lowered and the family started to get to their feet. The rain began again.

Paul Anfield moved closer to the family standing around the shrine, hastily mumbling condolences and Good-To-See-You-Let's-Call-We-Should-See-Each-Other to the rest of those present. He hardly knew them, after all. Then he hurried to his car, realising that his Gucci loafers had been ruined by the wet grass. Style and rain don't go together, he reflected.

He sat in his car and waited until a number of cars had passed by. In his rear-view mirror he noted that one of the waiting limos, a black Mercedes S-class with plates from Dade County, Florida, had stopped. Its dark tinted windows did not allow a view of the interior.

One of the two Latin men was beside it, holding an umbrella. He opened the rear door of the Mercedes for the woman in red. The other man, standing behind the car, was scanning the other people. Then he hurried to a car following the Benz. He looked on the alert, as if he expected some unknown enemy or danger.

The doors of the other car quickly closed and pulled away with its headlights and tail lights ablaze. The two men got into a dark blue Jeep Cherokee, also with tinted windows and also on Florida licence plates, which accelerated away to catch up with the Merc.

Bodyguards, or at least people in the personal security business, concluded Paul. Yet Lewman, Applebaum and Fromm were hardly the kind of lawyers who had clients in need of such protection. Surely Uncle Lenny wouldn't either – would he?

He wiped away the rain from his forehead and chin. He would probably find out in the office tomorrow.

INTRODUCTION

The drive back to Manhattan was slow, thanks to the rain. And every few miles the traffic kept stopping. An unusually large number of cars seemed to be breaking down and having to be pushed to the side by their owners.

CHAPTER 1

New York

The offices of Lewman, Applebaum and Fromm were in a typical office tower off Park Avenue, near 55th Street. The black marble building housed 45 floors of offices, homes to a group of people who came every day to justify their salaries or look for a step upwards in their self-imposed struggle towards whatever they had set their sights on. You could change the nameplates of the companies inside, but the building and the people working there every day would still be the same.

The information age was eating away at people like this, everywhere in the business world. Their physical presence was becoming less and less necessary. Soon it wouldn't be needed at all. For any company, it made more sense to let the workers do their stuff at home through PCs, faxes, phones and the web, without renting expensive space in Manhattan, or anywhere else. And then there was the saving in transport...

These were the thoughts that were going through Paul Anfield's mind as he rode the elevator up to the 40th floor, the lowest of the 10 floors occupied by Lewman, Applebaum and Fromm.

Lewmans represented more than 40 years of New York uptown and downtown legal history, for anybody who was anyone in business or society. The firm had consistently worked in one capacity or another for firms from the Fortune 500 list of companies. It catered perfectly for this economy-shaping group of worldwide entities. Its owners, its interests and its social structures even extended to divorce proceedings, though these were handled through trusted third parties.

It was a Teflon firm. Dirt never stuck. Everything could be negotiated, once the money was in place.

Jenny and Lisa-Maria, the Lewman front-desk team, were the first point of contact for anyone going through the main entrance on the 40th floor. They were busy as usual that morning.

'Lewman, Applebaum and Fromm, good morning. How can we help you? Let me put you through to Mr Robinson's secretary – he's out on a visit to Miami but his PA is aware that you were going to call – hold on and let me put you through.'

'Lewman, Applebaum and Fromm, good morning… yes, you are correct, the papers are here in our offices. No – sorry, but you will need to come by personally or send somebody empowered by you.'

'You would need to speak to Jane Robards, she is in charge of this matter on behalf of Adolf Neumann who is travelling in Europe, please hold on….'

Jenny looked up as Paul entered. She had six messages for him. Turning left into the main corridor, his Hartmann attaché case and raincoat in his right hand, he had already started reading them.

'Hi, Paul!'

'Morning Joanna, and let me guess - could I please go up to the 43rd and see David right away?'

'Who else would the managing senior partner want to speak at this hour of the morning but the most brilliant young lawyer around this part of town?' answered a laughing Joanna Palukai, secretary to David Fromm.

'Tell him I'll be there in 15 minutes' said Paul.

His office was not small – it just looked that way, thanks to the quantities of papers stacked up in every available space, including the floor around his desk. The walls carried the only personal touch in the room, a quartet of oil paintings by the 17th century Sicilian painter Pietro Novelli, a gift from Paul's father Robert when he had started his career. They were landscapes of the area around Bivona, south of Corleone on the island of Sicily. Bivona had been the birthplace of Paul's grandfather, Giuseppe Caruna, on his mother Carla's side of his family.

Giuseppe had met his future wife towards the end of the fighting in Sicily, while stationed in Palermo during the Second World War. Anfield senior had worked for US Army intelligence and was a link man with local island politicians and La Cosa Nostra. For a long time this had been secret from the public, but now it was part of history.

The relationship between the US Government and the Mafia had been carefully explained and exhaustively analysed over the past 50 years. Essentially, collaboration with organised crime had been necessary to save the lives of as many US soldiers as possible. Wars always demonstrated that strange relationships were normal when one party needed local support and another could provide it. Moral judgements were for peacetime.

The Mafia arranged for a number of local Sicilian contacts to function almost as liaison officers for the US military. This meant of course that the military commanders were expected to look the other way when the Mafia organised an economic return for its efforts. Their ill-gotten gains were, of course, forgotten. Forever.

But Giuseppe and Robert Anfield, a colonel of the US infantry who had been in charge of local relations at the highest levels, got off to a shaky start. Giuseppe Caruna didn't like anyone who didn't come from the island. Nothing personal, just the custom of the time and the place. Add to this the fact that Giuseppe had three beautiful daughters whom he protected with the vengeance typical of Sicily and its family culture.

Grandfather Giuseppe and his four brothers represented one of the most influential clans on the island, at least outside the larger towns. Robert Anfield knew this. He and Giuseppe finally struck a practical deal, one whose details had always remained hidden from Paul and everybody else in the family.

The marriage between Paul's parents was a shining example of how happiness should look in the long run. His upbringing and that of his brothers had been one of stable values. You lived within the rules and expectations. You were allowed some 'gambling' with experiences on the fringes, and if the gambling went wrong, you spoke to your family, who were there to help and guide. It gave Paul and his brothers and sisters an inner strength and peace in life.

Not a day passed for Paul when the colours of the paintings failed to bring memories back of summers spent as a child on his grandfather's estate. Neither his daily work nor New York's summer, winter, spring or autumn weather would influence how he started the day. The colours of the Novelli paintings would warm his day, shape his mood. The orange sunset or the blue sky, the yellow glow of corn in a field as Novelli had seen it, could change any mood.

Paul checked a number of notes that had been left for him, picked up the phone and called David Fromm's office to tell him he would there in five minutes. In the meantime, his new Sony VAIO PC zoomed into life. The computer's revolutionary personal page layout gave him news, financial markets and the message system of the firm, as well as setting out his daily agenda.

Routinely he connected his Nokia cell phone to his VAIO to update his agenda, so that when he returned from his meeting with David Fromm he would immediately be ready to go.

CHAPTER 2

Paul stepped away from his cluttered desk and went out of his room, down the hallway and up the steps of the connecting internal office staircase. On the stairs he met Richard Dunkin, one of the other senior managing partners.

'Did you get any joy out of Motorola the other day on the Blackfin hedge fund approach?' Richard asked him.

'Hi. No, nothing' Paul answered.

Both men laughed. They had known each other too long to be bothered about this.

'Means they are on their own on this one. Lunch or squash?'

'Lunch – let me know where.' Paul moved on.

'Hey!'

Paul turned. 'You OK?

'You know, it was your Uncle Lenny who brought me here after Harvard, raised me here, helped me make it here. I'll miss him.'

They looked at each other.

'Thanks, Richie – we'll raise a glass to him during lunch. That's the place where he did the big ones!'

They both laughed again. Lenny Gerstner had a 60/40 rule: 60 percent paperwork, file knowledge, intellectual fireworks etc, but it was the 40 percent where it really happened. As Lenny said, the 60 percent was basics, anybody could do that if they put their mind to it. The other 40 percent was the art of a deal.

Paul reached David Fromm's offices and waited. Hivani, his Indian secretary, smiled and signalled to him go in through the open door of the office.

David Fromm's office was tasteful but in powerbroker style. It was a large corner office with floor to ceiling windows, modern paintings on two walls, four silent plasma TV screens with stations from four different time zones, a big working table stacked with documents and a writing table on the side where he did his work. He had worked standing up since he had joined the firm after graduating from Harvard, because of a severe back problem which made it impossible for him to work sitting down. It was the result of a freak accident during his final year at Harvard, when he had been hit by a car crossing the road as he was coming back from a rowing session. He forgot to check for traffic and was hit by the van carrying the boats for the Harvard rowing team for the next week's regatta. He had tried yoga and pilates as well as two hours of exercises every day to try to keep back working and his body off the painkillers. His reaction to the injury said a lot about his character.

David had taken over from Lenny Gerstner as Managing Partner five years before at the age of 49, when Lenny had decided it was time for Lewman, Applebaum and Fromm to start doing business the modern way. The changes called for a young, driven and savvy new managing partner. Gerstner and the other senior partners had quickly picked up on the fact that either you had offices and local partners in the top business markets of London, Paris, Tokyo and the other world capitals or you took the decision to focus on New York.

The fact that David's great-grandfather was one of the founding partners had helped win him the job. David might have been only the second Fromm to have joined the firm, but he had been fundamental in its development. David had that extra intellectual ability.

As Paul walked in, David Fromm, six feet five inches tall, a head full of grey curls and with the face of Henry Fonda, was standing behind his writing desk, absorbed in his computer. He was holding his mobile phone to his ear. The jacket of his dark blue handmade Paul Stuart suit hung as usual over one of the chairs around the oval meeting table. Paul had only ever seen David in a white or light blue shirt with a polka dot tie in red, white or blue.

'Hi – just a sec' said David. He waved his hand in greeting. Paul walked to the window and enjoyed its spectacular view of New York in sunshine.

Fromm put his hand over the phone and half whispered: 'On the meeting table behind you, a grey folder with the name Kaneko Holdings - have a look while I finish this.'

Paul turned from the window and walked over to the table to look for the file among a heap of papers in all shapes and sizes. With so much paper around, no wonder lawyers had to bill in hours and took so long to come to the point.

He found the file and sat down to look at it. It had been compiled by his Uncle Lenny. A cover note directed the partnership to further executive action, including law enforcement agencies.

Paul frowned. That was not something his uncle would usually have put on file. He flipped the first page and started reading.

By the time he had been reading for 10 minutes, his mouth had turned dry and his head was spinning.

'I'll get us some water and Coke' said Fromm, looking at Paul's face. 'Yes, I was as surprised as you are.'

'Where did you get this? And when?' said Paul.

'It came by DHL at 10.45 last night. I've already tried to check through DHL who the sender was, but they only could say it was a walk-in at the Lennox Street DHL branch near Wall Street – they paid in cash, no return address, nothing'.

Fromm stepped away from his writing table and walked over to the window.

'This document must have been released the moment Lenny's death became official. And although the file covers more than 25 years, Lenny knew exactly who he wanted to send it to - you and me. To you because you're family and to me because of the logical link with the firm and its partners. Perhaps you'd better read it all through first, and than we can talk.'

Paul started to get up.

'You'd better do the reading here, until we can decide what we should do' said Fromm. 'It gets worse towards the end.'

Fromm returned to his standing desk. 'Paul, did your uncle Lenny ever mention anything of this?'

'No – never. He never mentioned Kaneko.'

'What I did know – and you all knew – was that he had a number of international relationships which he brought with him when the partnership was founded. You remember those long dinners when all those guys came over from Europe or wherever? They showed up at the office, then he took them off to some restaurant or the Plaza, The Pierre or wherever they were staying.'

Fromm looked at Paul from behind his desk, then turned and went to the window. The New York sky was changing. Rain was expected in Manhattan during the late afternoon.

'If this gets out we won't be able to contain it' said Fromm. 'The FBI, SEC or NSA or some other agency are going to analyse every page of the file you're holding, the names involved, the accounts, the cashflow – everything.' He softened his voice and chuckled.

'Lenny Gerstner, founding partner of New York's oh-so-respectable Lewman, Applebaum and Fromm, the leading law firm for corporate USA, was also lawyer to one of the biggest undeclared money pools around, with the active collaboration of people directly connected to the US Government.'

Paul wanted to react to this remark but he said nothing. Now was not the time.

Fromm attended to more calls while Paul continued to skim through the document. He filtered out certain passages and remarks. Fromm gave him 20 minutes before speaking again.

'Good – action!' he said. 'What are we going to do, Paul? Or better - what do you want to do?'

Paul stood up and walked over to join Fromm at the window.

'We need time' Paul answered. 'Time to think about what we'll do with this, both internally and of course externally. Do you agree?'

David turned and looked at Paul. 'I can give you until four o'clock, when we have the bi-weekly partners' meeting. Come and see me before and we'll prepare matters accordingly.' Every second Monday of each month, Lewman, Applebaum and Fromm had a partners' meeting when they discussed relevant issues.

Paul turned and walked towards the door.

'Paul?'

Paul turned.

'The firm is the key concern – your uncle always understood that. We're OK on this?'

Paul waited a beat. 'Sure' he said. That veiled warning meant he was on his own. Nothing personal, just healthy professional self-preservation. Fromm and the other partners wouldn't think twice about cutting Paul loose if it would safeguard them from any situation threatening their livelihoods, or more importantly the social and professional status and esteem that went with them.

And one thing was clear from what he had read - they had a ticking time-bomb on their hands.

A leading lawyer had been covering up for a US Government-sponsored scheme whereby past political 'demons' - stopping communism spreading throughout the US backyard of Latin America – had thought it best to go via a conduit whose character had not been seen as unduly threatening at the time – narcotics. They had been shipping weapons to the area, then turning a blind eye on the so-called 'empty' planes flying back stateside, which quickly became filled with 'goods'. The drugs were being brought into the US via guarded semi-military airstrips.

CHAPTER 3

Madrid, early summer 1993

Juanita Diaz was already unconscious when she hit the wall. Blood spurted freely from her nose and eyebrows. Caesar Biesca grunted and sweated with the effort of hitting her. The level of alcohol in his blood had blocked his mind. Again.

Juanita's naked body had become a punchbag for the Vice President of the Board of Banco Industrial de Iberica, or BANINSA as it was known in Spain. His right foot struck the girl as she flopped back from the wall.

It was all because ten minutes earlier, Biesca had failed to get an erection after one of his famous lunches in one of the boardrooms of the bank. If he wasn't travelling on a Tuesday or Friday he was driven after lunch to the chalet in La Moraleja, a well-known residential area outside Madrid, owned by the bank and used for private meetings and the entertainment of the President and a number of selected board members.

Juanita Diaz lay on the floor, not moving. Blood spots had showered the floor round her head.

'Stupid cunt!' sneered Biesca, turning around and stumbling to look for his shirt.

The room's windows were closed. It smelled of sweat, traces of cheap perfume and unconsummated sex.

Biesca sat on a chair, his bowed head looking down at the cause of his alcohol-driven rage - his own limp penis.

How ridiculous, he thought – Caesar Biesca could get involved in any business venture in the country, but he couldn't get his own dick up.

He found his shirt underneath the chair and pulled it on, without making the effort to fasten the buttons. Then he looked for his pants.

The girl still didn't move, and her blood was now spreading across the white marble floor. Biesca's alcohol-driven mind seemed to slow down at the sight of the girl and he felt a sudden instinct to get away from the place.

Juanita Diaz had not been able to arouse him with either her hands or her mouth. Biesca, when under the influence of alcohol, was swift in his mood swings and completely unpredictable in his violence.

In the mornings, he was a highly experienced and competent banker. After lunch - it was a different matter.

Biesca's career spanned working in government as an Under Secretary of Trade, then becoming Senior Vice President at Petroleos de España. Now he was Executive Vice President of the Board of BANINSA, the second largest bank in Spain, under the guidance of his long-time friend Ramon Diaz, the most gifted entrepreneur in Spanish finance and industry.

Diaz and Biesca had been friends since their student days. Diaz had the human attributes of top intellect, discipline and luck, combined with an all-consuming ambition when it was needed.

Biesca, like so many of his friends, had floated through life. Life for him had been mapped out. His family was a steady provider of ministers and other leading public figures in society, and his mother's side had brought wealth. He had immediately detected Ramon's superior brainpower.

Biesca pulled up his pants. He heard a soft knock at the door.

'Señor Biesca, por favor - open the door! Don César, por favor - abre!'

It was the voice of the head of his four bodyguards. They had called the BANINSA HQ requesting orders, as the matter was clearly getting out of hand.

One man came immediately - Javier Sanchez, a decorated ex-captain of the Guardia Civil, trained by MOSSAD operatives and head of security for BANINSA. He spent practically all his waking hours as the security guardian for President Ramon Diaz and his family. Sanchez was probably the only person who knew at every moment where Ramon Diaz was, what he was doing, where he was going.

Juanita Diaz still did not move. The gurgling had stopped.

The room was a sober white marbled-floor bedroom on the first floor of the chalet overlooking the lawn and swimming-pool. There were no colours, just black and white.

The girl had begun a striptease, and her skirt, panties and bra were still lying around.

Biesca slipped on his soft leather shoes, looking at the whitewashed walls, the white marble floor and the harsh red colour of Juanita's blood. He got up and walked stiffly to the door. The knocking had increased and the whispers behind it were now urgent.

Biesca unsteadily opened the door. Sanchez stepped urgently inside. Biesca didn't dare to look him in the eye.

Sanchez walked over to the girl, bent and slowly turned her over so that her beaten face came into full view.

He felt for the vein in her neck; there was a pulse, but it was irregular.

'Call Dr. Ibañez and send a car to bring him here! Ahora!' he shouted.

Juanita Diaz suddenly grunted, seeming to float back into a state of consciousness.

Her whole face was covered in blood. Some of it was already drying.

Biesca leaned against the open door, his red-rimmed eyes not registering the reality of the situation. He shook his head, mumbled something unintelligible and stumbled back into the room.

At the same moment, two cars stopped outside the house. From the smaller car following, two men came out, running to the big dark blue Audi A8 in front. One of them opened the rear door of the Audi; the tinted windows made it impossible to see who was inside.

The Chairman of BANINSA, Ramon Diaz, emerged from the car and crossed quickly to the main entrance of the house.

Diaz was dressed as he nearly always appeared in the press – a dark blue hand-made suit, a white shirt and a matching crisp white handkerchief loosely folded in the breast pocket of his suit and a heavy silk dark blue Ferragamo tie with a pattern of small white elephants. He looked every inch the established Spanish powerbroker.

He had spoken already to Sanchez, who had called him as soon as he had received the message from Biesca's head of security.

He entered the hall and surveyed the functional décor. The house was exclusively used to host selected events. It was the place where the bank held so called 'off-sites' - events which were exclusive to board members. Conversations with investors, meetings with key BANINSA shareholders, certain meetings with political leaders, all those meetings which need to take place away from HQ but not at someone's private house.

The caretaker and one of the security team showed Diaz up the stairs. They passed several rooms before finding Biesca. The vice-president in the meantime had sat down and more or less finished dressing.

The girl on the floor had now curled herself into a ball and was softly crying. No-one had thought to cover up her nakedness.

'Please take Sr. Biesca home and put him to bed, now' said Ramon Diaz. He spoke with a natural authority. No clarification or questions were needed.

Sanchez and another man gently drew Caesar Biesca to his feet and led him out of the room. Biesca did not dare to look into the eyes of his friend as he passed him.

'Is Dr Ibañez on his way?' Diaz asked Sanchez, taking care that only he could hear him.

'He will be here within 20 minutes.'

'Sanchez, please sort this out with the girl or her family. No details, no talking to friends, press or anything. Please make them understand that we deeply regret this matter, but that all involved are better off forgetting it and we hope that an economic incentive would help matters. Clear? '

'Si, señor.'

Diaz sat down, and Sanchez left the room.

Caesar Biesca's increased alcohol abuse seemed to go hand in hand with the problems of the BANINSA Group. The stories, led by La Union Hispania, which had started to appear in the daily papers in both Madrid and Barcelona about three months before, had clearly been aimed at bringing down Ramon Diaz and his friends at BANINSA.

The stories all came back from one source. The leading socialist party members both in and outside government were not at all pleased with the overbearing presence of Diaz. Hailed by the people, loathed by the political forces – this was Spain, as it always was and always would be.

La Union Hispania was Spain's largest newspaper group, owned by the ASIPR conglomerate, whose family shareholders had been very much at the forefront of helping the Socialist government to attain power after the death of General Franco. And BANINSA had problems; Spain had been in economic crisis ever since the 1992 Barcelona Olympic Games and the Seville World Fair. Clients of BANINSA had had trouble paying back the loans they had taken out since then.

CHAPTER THREE

The stock price was under great pressure, and a capital increase was vital to keep the BANINSA machine going. Or to be more precise, to keep the Inspectors of the Banco de España, the regulator bank, at bay. On top of this, the crucial sale of BANINSA's industrial holdings had gone much too slowly, thanks to Saddam Hussein and the Gulf War.

All these carefully-orchestrated corporate situations – corporate problems - suddenly started to bite, thanks to the ever-present Spanish press.

Diaz looked one more time around the room, then went down through the spacious living area and out on to the terrace. The garden of the chalet was screened by trees and a fence prevented people from looking in. The beautifully-maintained, secluded garden was silent except for the incessant chirruping of the crickets, so inextricably linked with the heat of Spain.

Diaz walked towards the table and chairs which stood beside the pool in the centre of the garden. He sat down, took out a cigarette and searched for a light. Finally, from the inside of his jacket, he dug out a golden Du Pont lighter and lit his cigarette.

Blowing out the smoke, he read the worn text engraved on the top of the lighter: VIRTUVIO 1990. He put the lighter back in his jacket.

Ramon Diaz always knew that history could not be changed. The scene he had just witnessed was another sign that matters were spinning out of control. His mind wandered back through time.

CHAPTER 4

History

The Virtuvio Group had been formed by Pedro Cortes' grandfather. It had consisted of construction companies, a discount supermarket chain active all over Spain and South America and the largest network of filling stations on Spanish territory. Diaz had joined the Cortes family as their lawyer and had swiftly become CEO while the group was struggling to find its future. He had surrounded himself with a trusted group of collaborators, all hand-picked, most of them known to him from his days at the University of Salamanca.

This was his trademark: a small group of professionals led by him, no questions asked, no intruders - full control. It was also the beginning of the end of Diaz' personal relationship with Pedro Cortes. Cortes, as President of the Board and other core shareholders and Board Members of the Virtuvio Group, was constantly kept in the dark by the brilliant moves made by the CEO and his team. Results were impressive, a fact which was acknowledged in the press and at the annual shareholders' meeting.

Since he had taken over the running of the group, Diaz had used American-style business tactics, unknown in Spain at the beginning of the 1980s. This meant a mixture of heavy cost-cutting, new products, increased sales per employee and aggressive takeover strategies in building up the core activities of the Group, all supported by a huge IT investment. The result was doubled group sales volumes and more profit for distribution to the shareholders. This ideal situation had kept Pedro Cortes and his family in control of more than 60% of the voting stock.

The difference was however always there: the Cortes family had had money and style for more than two centuries, while Ramon Diaz was the son of a village doctor from the north of Spain. He had no money and no style, just two basic ingredients which would always make him a No. 1 - brains and guts. He also had unparalleled natural arrogance.

It was the brains-and-guts combination which had attracted Pedro Cortes from the beginning. And what a good partnership it had been; young Pedro Cortes had to take over a run-down family empire, while his real interest was in living the life which he had always known, one dictated by the seasons. His study of economics was combined with sun-related activities like sailing, tennis, golf and skiing. Away from the summer months there was hunting, either at the family-owned Sierra Blanco or at one of the other estates – fincas in Spanish - owned by friends of the Cortes family.

Pedro Cortes knew that one day he was going to face the real test - the taking over of the management of the Virtuvio Group.

Cortes' father had died in 1978, the year before Spain joined the EEC. Pedro had his first formal meeting as President and CEO and met his fellow board members for the first time in an official situation. They were all trusted friends of his father or grandfather in a world based on courtesy, style and insider knowledge which had no place for an outsider, however professionally or otherwise qualified.

The facts and figures showed that either drastic action had to be taken to revitalise the family group or Virtuvio would become a takeover target within the Spanish market in the build-up to joining the EEC. The day-to-day management at that time were all people loyal to Virtuvio, according to the values instilled by Pedro Cortes' father and his father before him - you came to work, while all the decision making was made by the owner. So when Pedro Cortes came home after that first historic board meeting, he knew one thing - a new board and management team for Virtuvio had to be found as fast as possible.

The board members were not a problem. They were all old men, and the death of Pedro's father gave them a good moment to retire. Virtuvio's board was in that sense typical of the Spanish model at that time - becoming a member of such a board was seen as a final social and professional accolade after a dedicated business life, usually in one way or the other connected to such a company.

There was always one golden rule - all decisions taken or approved involved supporting the President of the Board in anything and everything. You weren't appointed to the board to think or act independently. Given also that international institutional investors were then not really known in the Spanish economy, this system kept the real power of Spanish companies well controlled. The big problem lay in finding a true manager and management team to put Virtuvio back on course.

Pedro Cortes had made a few phone calls that night. Mainly they were to old university contacts and business people he knew who had similar ideas about what was needed in such cases. All of them shared the huge changes Spain and its business community were going to face at the time of joining the united Europe, the EEC.

By the time he went to bed that night, Pedro had three names. The next day his sources had taken care that appointments would be made over the next few weeks. Two of the names proved to be unreachable; one was working with a large bank and on the verge of being named Governor of the Bank of Spain. The other was due to join the board of a foreign multinational and was not willing to entertain the idea of joining Virtuvio, because of the family character of the group.

The third name had been the one that had triggered Cortes's interest

- Ramon Diaz. Diaz was at that time a partner at a well-known law firm specialising in corporate finance practice.

During the following weeks Cortes had met several times with Diaz, first during a lunch organized by the senior partner of the firm Diaz was working and then either at Cortes' office or in the lobby of the Ritz Hotel. After their third meeting, Cortes knew he had found the man to put Virtuvio back on track.

Diaz did not leave his law firm without an unwritten promise to keep in close contact. In other words, when a law firm was required at Virtuvio it was clear which one would get preferential treatment.

In the years that followed, Virtuvio started to grow, concentrating on a number of core activities - food & beverages and construction. The gas stations, the shares in agricultural projects, real estate, industrial participations in various conglomerates, were all sold to finance growth and acquisitions.

Virtuvio was turned from a run-down family vehicle into a thriving company. Diaz always had two things clear in mind, profit and growth, which expanded his own personal power and interests at the same time.

To make the most profit and keep on its growth strategy, the group needed at a certain point to take the decision either to sell a large equity share to third parties, or the Diaz idea: to become a public company, an IPO. In Spain at the time, the stock exchange was very small and controlled by daily trading flows. There were no local institutional investors to give liquidity to a market. The Spanish stock markets – Madrid, Barcelona, Valencia and Bilbao – were mainly moved by foreign investors and the local banks or groups connected to them.

The real reason for Diaz to take the IPO route was a more direct one: Virtuvio was owned by Pedro Cortes and his family through a family holding company. Pedro was the only male, and running the day-today management of such a company meant an obligation to get results when you were 51% in control.

Pedro's four sisters had become Diaz's natural enemies from the day they were presented. The four sisters knew by feminine intuition that Ramon Diaz only cared in the end about Ramon Diaz, and that the family was just a stepping stone. They tried to bring their brother Pedro around to their point of view. Pedro Cortes' answer had been unchanged: 'You are not able to run this company. Be happy that every year you receive your dividends. Since Diaz has taken over the management, look how the share price has gone up.'

This was a typical answer by a dominant male family member in the Spain of this time, whenever a woman offered an opinion. But Pedro Cortes knew that once he had handed the effective running of the company to Diaz, there was no way back. If Diaz were in charge, he would always become, and remain, Number One.

If Cortes had inherited one thing, it had been a unique ability to read people within five minutes of looking at them and listening to them. When Diaz became CEO, the present and future changed, for both Virtuvio and Cortes.

The very first board meeting with Diaz in attendance resulted in the complete and total turnover of all the members. This of course was prepared and handled by Cortes; these tired old men had not produced any tangible results for the company in real economic terms. In Spain however, such a revolution had great social impact.

On top of this commotion – and commented on heavily at the time by the Spanish financial press - were the names of the new Virtuvio Board members, proposed by Diaz and backed by the sole shareholder, Pedro Cortes. The personal friendships, the professional background, the age of each one, tied the whole group directly to Diaz.

Diaz had found the two ingredients for rapid growth – national and international financial services groups and related investors with willingness to finance, and local companies in need of such finance, plus the centralised management Diaz and the Virtuvio team brought in mergers and acquisitions transactions.

But Diaz and his friends got results. Virtuvio broke $500 million turnover within three years of the changes, with profits of over 20% for its shareholders. Spain was catching up after the damage to the economy done during and after the Franco years.

These figures effectively triggered the last part of the Diaz strategy. Virtuvio was to become a public company through an IPO - an initial public offering, or as some stockbrokers liked to call it, an 'Idiots Please Order'.

Diaz had been preparing this step for some time. Contrary to a lot of other Spanish entrepreneurs with a natural distrust of informing any shareholder outside their control, he had the experience and the knowledge of the investment banking business community; the ones who were going to do the real work, the very same ones who so willingly had financed its growth.

During his days as a lawyer, Diaz had been involved in various takeovers, IPOs and other such operations and had always studied the 'flow', as he called it. He explained the term to Cortes one grey day at Barcelona Airport. The word consisted of several ingredients. You needed a favourable economic climate, the stock markets locally and abroad should be at high levels, and PR companies should have been active during the previous year creating an image for the company through any means of press coverage and in any format. The company should be actively courting banks, brokers - again locally and abroad - and feeding them all the same message: to run the IPO would mean prestige, income and fat personal bonuses.

Diaz knew exactly what all the 'ingredients' were. He knew how to make them function as the 'flow'.

The extra factor, as he explained to Cortes, had already been created. The flow was greatly strengthened by the general interest in Spain from abroad at that time. The country was going to organise the world EXPO in Seville and the Olympic Games in Barcelona, and needed investment in everything related to infrastructure. Smooth political change given the economic growth since the death of Franco and the entrance of Spain into the EEC.

In a word - Spain and the Spanish economy were hot. And they were going to heat up further.

International investors who were used to large and liquid position-taking in equity and bond investments were anxious to invest. Diaz called this the GCC - the Goat Club Complex. Nobody in the investment industry wanted to miss the big feast called Spain and this meant (as would be proven later) that investment discipline, accurate due diligence processes and standards, was lowered.

Being in the right place at the right time with the right deal was subject to speed and to spur-of-the-moment decision-making - just like goats charging into in a new pasture. However, Spain and its stock markets were too small at that time - position building in Spanish blue chip stocks meant at that time an operation of weeks. Otherwise, the investor would drive up the price through his own stock purchases.

Diaz also knew that such an exercise was one of timing. And that, he told Cortes, was the real good part of his strategy - at least until after the 1992 Olympic Games plus the closing of Seville's World Fair, the reality for investments in Spain would be undisputed.

Afterwards, Spain and its Government should start paying all those who financed this extraordinary expansion and events.

CHAPTER 5

Virtuvio started as a pre-IPO project in the spring of 1989, directed by Diaz personally in a whirlwind of visits in London, New York and Tokyo, aimed at raising the profile. All contacts with banks, brokers and lawyers in all those places were consulted, questioned and coaxed, with one main aim: to prepare in record time a profile and name recognition in all the major financial circles who controlled in the end the ultimate step of lining up potential investors prepared to buy shares in Virtuvio.

This first step brought Diaz and his team the result he had promised to Pedro Cortes - the large investment banks and PR agencies came calling in Madrid to seduce Virtuvio as a client.

Diaz knew exactly why they would come. If a Spanish company with such a high-profile chairman and sales in the region of more than $500 million was willing to discuss its fat fees for a world-wide IPO, then Madrid was the place to come for an urgent meeting with the President and Board of Virtuvio.

The selection process for Virtuvio and the Diaz team was really a reverse play, and typical of Diaz - playing at the 'me-too' attitude of these banks and the short-term-only money-driven interest of their managers. All the major banks appeared at the Virtuvio offices in Madrid to make their pitch. Diaz's team during this so-called 'beauty contest' only had to sit back, release certain types of information to create confusion and insecurity and make them ready for the finish.

Two things were achieved: the potential contenders became more aggressive, with some of them falling out of the race. The mandate had been manipulated into something much bigger than it really was, but Diaz and the Virtuvio team knew the important thing at that time for these foreign investment banks was to score in the new and lucrative Spanish market.

As the last three banks placed their bids with the Virtuvio board the prices of services started to drop. By then Pedro Cortes had already stopped being amazed at the aggressiveness of the game plan Diaz had planned and was executing. He and Diaz were constantly approached, invited, consulted by banks, their lawyers, supposed independent consultants and all interested in the IPO of Virtuvio - directly or indirectly, through friends and foes. Everybody wanted to land the big one.

This second step was finished within four months. The winner was the banking group Diaz and Cortes felt was the most prestigious of the lot, Rheinman Partners. Rheinman would arrange a worldwide syndicate of financial institutions to underwrite the Virtuvio issue.

Given its need to stay on top or as much as possible, the Virtuvio deal was priced for its fees as if Virtuvio was an AAA German or English quoted company, but the reasons the senior Rheinman Partners gave was valid: the key thing was to get into the Spanish market with such a high-profile deal. Other deals would come to them and fatter fees would then be charged.

The final discussions with the Rheinman people were handled directly by Cortes and Diaz on a Saturday in early March 1990 on the Cortes finca Sierra Blanco; a day Cortes would never forget. The 90,000 hectare Sierra Blanco, one hour south of Jaen, had been in the Cortes family for over 250 years. Its main house, Cortijo, was one of the most beautiful in Spain. Having lunch or dinner in its courtyard, one became drugged by the scent of lemon trees, olives and flowers and the unique air of Andalucía.

Thus was the setting for a final meeting of minds between the leaders. That Saturday morning everyone involved started to show up between 11 and 12 o'clock. Rheinman people, Virtuvio's team, lawyers and the contracted PR organisation.

'Buenos Diaz everybody!'

Diaz strode forward from the back of the open courtyard, where about 25 people were seated casually dressed behind three large wooden tables, arranged in a U shape and with several easels in front to carry drawings, points of reference and other documents.

Diaz, as always, was impeccably dressed; an image which had also been carefully projected over these last months in the national and international press.

'On behalf of ourselves personally and the Virtuvio Board, we thank you all for the work and effort done to prepare our project - the IPO of our group. Today and tomorrow we will finalise our final game plan.

'Pedro Cortes and I feel we have brought together the most outstanding group of professionals to achieve this.' Diaz looked at the team leaders present.

'The size of this IPO is unique for Spain and the Spanish economy, so we have no room to fail. Virtuvio is to set the standard for Spain as a step towards a leading role within Europe. That's our project and that is what we want to share with our new shareholders, ladies and gentlemen.'

After lunch, the rough draft of conditions for the IPO was agreed by all parties involved, though with the knowledge that 15 or more drafts would need to be passed before it could be send to the CNMV – Spain's SEC - for filing.

Rheinman's senior partner and CEO for Europe, Peter Morales, who was in charge of this operation, took the stand.

'We would like to propose that a final timetable is produced not later than three weeks from today. We have been sounding out the market through our organisation and others. Reactions from our main clients and other institutional investors are good. Based on these reactions, we have formed an initial consortium of underwriters for the issue, and we are proud to say that all the major international banks in the European, US and Far East markets have indicated to us both verbally and in writing that they wish to participate. This means we have achieved a new record for a book-running operation for a Spanish company.'

The reaction to his words was typical of these professionals – hushed enthusiasm. It was simple logic: if Rheinman lent its name to such an IPO, in normal economic market conditions this would mean the IPO issue would be comfortably over-subscribed, guaranteeing the underwriters of the shares instant benefits at practically zero risk.

Already then, Rheinman and its partners were on a clear path to becoming the absolute reference worldwide when talking about finance. Over the years a number of past and present Rheinman partners would become presidents, CEOs, board members and cabinet ministers in the US administration.

Cortes smiled and looked at Diaz sitting beside him. It was Diaz who had taken care to make sure that after careful screening of all possible and potential investment banks, the most respectable one came on top.

Rheinman's interest would be used to enter the Spanish market in its usual style to become the No. 1 investment bank in Europe in the shortest time possible. This meant in their world only one thing: size. Size for the deal, the market, the partnership and personal prestige and the most important one: the impact on their year end bonus for the Rheinman partners involved.

Diaz had an easy time preparing the ground for this vital step. Virtuvio, thanks largely to Diaz himself, was constantly being featured in the Spanish press. Any and all financial services companies were drawn to Virtuvio, its president and his style, practically fighting to achieve personal contact with Diaz or at least those near to him.

Once all the major financial services houses, directly or indirectly, had showed their interest in the Spanish market by sitting down for business with Virtuvio and its president, Diaz continued his beauty contest tactic with round no. 2, as so well explained by him to Cortes: find the most interesting ones and measure their greed.

For the last round, as Cortes called it, a simple technique was used: the last three parties, including Rheinman, had by then been worked on for more than six months by them and Virtuvio team. This meant relatively little effort for Virtuvio as a company at that stage, but the banks and investment banking departments of others were obliged to prove their worth to Virtuvio's president and board by giving presentations, sending in teams to investigate the Spanish market (new to all of them at that time at an in-depth level) and initiating contacts with the end investors, institutional investors who were needed to buy the Virtuvio shares in the IPO as a clear signal to the retail market.

Two weeks later in Madrid, Diaz and Cortes gave Rheinman the final piece of candy, the ultimate demonstration of faith for Virtuvio's IPO. Diaz and Cortes had made no secret of their intention to buy an important stake with Virtuvio in one of Spain's many banks. Given the relative delicacy of such an operation, Diaz had been preparing this for some time with the Rheinman CEO in Europe, Peter Morales, and his team.

Peter Morales was a Mexican by birth, the result of a happy and stable marriage between a Colombian father and an English mother. He was the typical Rheinman partner in all its glory. After primary school in Mexico and boarding school in Switzerland he had gone to Harvard, finished law cum laude at the top of his class and had captained its rowing club. He had gone on to enter INSEAD at Fontainebleau and had been head-hunted by Rheinman before even being interviewed by JP Morgan, Shell or any of the other big companies which wanted to seduce people like him.

Morales blended very easily into the introduction period at Rheinman and quickly climbed the professional ladder. He became a partner before his 35th birthday, Rheinman still firmly being a partnership, although the first stirrings were developing regarding the intellectual struggle over how to keep profits, expansion and partner quality at an even footing.

More importantly, Peter Morales had learned one very specific mantra at Rheinman. Founding partners and the first following generations of initial partners arrived at a simple and very powerful conclusion, which they applied increasingly over the years. They believed their markets and their clients had only three basic governing forces: the buyer, the seller and the man in the middle bringing them together. Rheinman became the house which very professionally amalgamated these three forces over time.

With this amalgamation they would always win, but in a very professional and disciplined way, always initially steering clear of the gatekeeper of ethical consciousness in the financial world: conflict of interest. Rheinman was going to fly over these conflicts of interest by being very consistent and always delivering. Only years later did regulatory bodies like the SEC start to catch up enough to supervise the financial markets.

Who better to serve the involved parties – ie the Government's Treasury Departments - by actively helping ex-Rheinman key people and partners to enter such entities?

All this, along with the ruthless discipline of team effort, ensured that Rheinman people were intellectually at the very top level. This meant logically that personal objectives were never on the table – Rheinman objectives were all that mattered. This was squared off at bonus time, or when partners were nominated, for those with intellectual patience and the ambition to match.

For Virtuvio the logic was clear - Spanish banks were still very large players in Spain's principal industrial companies. Spain joining the EEC would make the industrial stakes for those financial owners even more important.

So buying into a large bank carried logically a huge premium for entrance, given the powerhouses they were. If you were in one of them, you were sitting automatically on the board of various others, quoted or non-quoted but all sizeable for the Spanish economy.

After going through all the analysis with their teams, both men had settled their sights principally on one of Spain's oldest banks - BANINSA. Through his family holdings Cortes already had board membership of a number of companies where banks were heavily represented.

BANINSA was a perfect target for a party like Diaz and Cortes, with a large amount of cash to be raised from their Virtuvio IPO. The bank had a huge retail branch network and a very large number of industrial holdings in cement, oil, insurance, real-estate and many others, either quoted and or non-quoted. The importance of BANINSA was always quoted as reflecting in total about 3% of

Spain's GDP. Other banks and situations had been studied, discussed, tested and disregarded.

An irresolvable set of difficulties always seemed to appear when the alternatives were studied. Either there was one too-dominant shareholder – usually a family or similar – in place, or the company was too close to the description 'of national importance', meaning that the politicians would frustrate any intent. Another frequent problem was if a target was already quoted, so usually the free-float – the shares freely available via the stock exchange – was too small, meaning too long and costly a battle to win control. In addition, usually the company under attack could at relative leisure muster support from friends and family.

BANINSA had grown too big. Its shareholder base had become fragmented and the controlling families were at each others' throats, so large packages of shares could be acquired in a relatively short time. Spain's local SEC was not prepared to intervene, so operations at the level and size of a takeover for a BANINSA were driven forward by their own size and impact in combination with the people promoting them.

A divided BANINSA board, led by a CEO who was out of date and out of control, ensured it was in the position Diaz and Cortes had been waiting for. They knew that they had two very important opponents in trying to achieve success via a BANINSA type of operation – the so-called independent Banco de España, which was in fact strongly influenced by the leading political party and the established powerbrokers, in other words the families and related shareholders who kept strict control of the quoted companies by controlling their boards and management.

CHAPTER 6

The setting had been a lunch at one of the Jockey restaurant's private dining rooms with Rheinman's Peter Morales, some time in May 1992. This Madrid restaurant was and is a reflection of how top Spaniards went – and still go - about their business; very select and discreet on the one hand, but taking care that one is seen and acknowledged.

Even the layout reflected this – when you entered the main dining room at Jockey, you had could be directed to one of two areas. Either you went to the right-hand side or you were placed in the part in front of its serving bar. The first meant you and or the people inviting you 'belonged' there. The alternative was for those were simply not connected, or the people inviting them were foreigners who had only read about the restaurant.

If matters needed special care, one went up the stairs to the private dining rooms, which was where Diaz and Cortes had invited Morales to join them for lunch.

The fact that the restaurant was opposite the Internal Ministry and therefore in a street swamped by police and Guardia Civil agents gave it an additional appeal.

Anyone who was anyone in Spain had one external sign – private security men. The reason for personal security was the ever-present threat from ETA, the Basque armed independence organization.

When Diaz and Cortes entered Jockey they were welcomed by Carmelo, the restaurant's maître d' hôte, who had known them and their families personally for a very long time.

'Señores. Como estan?'

'Bien - gracias Carmelo. Has our guest arrived?' responded Diaz.

'Yes - he is waiting for you.'

Peter Morales was in one of the small dining rooms on the first floor of the restaurant. He got up when they entered the room.

Peter Morales was the London based CEO for Rheinman Partners in Europe. At 45 he looked, dressed and sounded like a recycled American. He was an investment banker; his clients were the reason he was no. 1. Not because of his clients, but in spite of them.

Morales was convinced that he was pretty close to being God's gift to mankind, but of course he was so well trained that he would never show it. It was just his natural place in the pecking order.

But men like Morales didn't really care for the likes of Diaz and Cortes. A top investment banker was primarily driven by a mixture of a very large ego, a ruthlessly egocentric outlook on life and the need always to follow the buck – in other words, his bonus potential.

When Morales had worked with the faceless and spineless CEOs of Europe's Financial Times 350 companies, without exception he had always had the upper hand. Such people were easy to deal with. They needed their jobs, and their jobs always had to show growth for their boards and shareholders. The M&A activities were needed to achieve it. Organic growth quickly became something from an old-and-slow past. You bought balance sheet size by buying and selling companies.

Internal M&A departments at such multinationals were always there to do deals through the likes of Peter Morales and Rheinman Partners. And nobody was ever fired for soliciting the services of the KPMG, BANINSA, McKinsey, Morgan Stanley - or Rheinman.

Clients like Diaz and Cortes were destabilizing; they knew what they were talking about, controlled their company boards of directors and as a result controlled the eventual fees their companies paid out through them. In addition, Diaz and Cortes were used to the service model – an advisor like Peter Morales, however well he was dressed, was just that – a commodity, an advisor.

Diaz and Cortes only had the wellbeing of their own business interests at heart, they didn't care about the people they had built their success with, and couldn't care less about a 'tombstone' – the famous post-deal ads financial services advisors always liked to put in the FT, Wall Street Journal, The Banker and similar. For Diaz and Cortes, Rheinman performed a service, however the service provider wanted to dress it up.

On the other hand, Peter Morales revelled intellectually in the fact that now and then he was able to work with people like Diaz and Cortes. It meant he really had to bring something extra to the table, knowing he was going to be challenged all along the way. He knew he was up against men who always kept people in front of them on the move, insecure. It was practically impossible to catch them off guard, yet they seemed to have a homing device whereby they always found, jointly or separately, the weakness in the opposite side.

So that, for Morales, was the setting for his lunch with the Virtuvio owners.

After the men had welcomed each other, a bottle of Marques Riscal Sauvignon, a top dry white wine from Valladolid, was immediately served, with a large plate of thinly sliced Jamon Iberico de Bellota: Spain's unbeatable combination, when starting a serious conversation.

'Thanks for meeting us at such short notice, Peter' said Diaz. 'We both felt that what we had to tell you is of vital importance for the IPO. Pedro?' Diaz left the explanation to his partner and began to enjoy the ham.

Cortes began. 'As we indicated to you and the other groups involved in this operation, we at Virtuvio felt it necessary to create a core shareholder group before launching the IPO. We also feel it should be very clear that we and our families will continue to lead the company from the front, not as financial investors.'

Morales had been born and educated in London, but he was half Cuban and therefore fluent in Spanish. His body language clearly indicated his interest in the words of Cortes.

'You and your team were aware that we had been talking to a variety of potential parties for some time' said Cortes. 'We are therefore very glad that we have reached final heads of agreement with our Italian partners the Cantarini group, one of the largest in food distribution in Italy, and Europe for that matter and our South American partners, the Lisker family, to financially support our IPO and cement the relations we have had with them over the years.'

Cortes took a sip of his white wine, savouring its quality. He put his glass down.

'To manage this, we, together with Cantarini and Lisker, have founded a new company, a Dutch BV holding company which will own 100% of Virtuvio voting shares and rights. The valuation agreed for their stakes is equal to the projected net worth pre-IPO of Virtuvio as was done by KPMG.'

Cortes continued to explain the involvement of the two groups mentioned and the financial aspects of the agreed operation. He gave some examples of his shared history, especially with the Cantarini family. Morales waited patiently until Cortes had ended his brief overview and put his first comments and professional observations on the table.

Through his and Rheinman's enormous sources, they had been aware that Diaz and Cortes had been talking to a number of very large family holdings and corporations and their owner's offices in a number of markets. It made common sense for Italians and South Americans to become involved with Spanish majority partners of the calibre of Diaz and Cortes.

Morales responded.

'As always, you two are able to amaze us all! Congratulations. We all know how this will further secure the IPO. Just a few questions to help me understand - in this Dutch BV vehicle, who will own what?'

'Diaz and I will have control with 51% of its shares, our partners the rest' said Cortes. 'The Dutch BV will hold 50.1% A shares and 49.9% shares will be the IPO via non-voting B shares. This NewCo will nominate six board seats of the 10 available on the Virtuvio Consejo.'

It was Morales' turn to taste the wine and enjoy its texture and flavour.

'I know the Cantarini group, but what I didn't know about is the interest of the Lisker family. The bank has had contacts with them but we never realised their interest in investment opportunities outside the US and South America.'

'Before I explain, let's order some food' answered Diaz as Carmelo, the maitre d'hôte, had softly entered the private dining room. The Jockey's famous sommelier Angel had also appeared at the table.

'Peter, would you still like the red wine we served the other day? Because I asked them to open up a special '83 magnum.'

Diaz smiled at the stylish way Cortes always knew what foreigners from whatever origin liked about him; small personal details as to what a person liked, in this case, the type of wine.

They ordered, and the wine – Mauro, a young bodega started in 1978 by the same man who had been responsible for the famous Vega Sicilia wines – was poured. Diaz continued, giving Cortes the chance to begin his starter.

'Javier Lisker feels as leader of his family-controlled group, just like us, that over the next 10 to 15 years Spain will become the natural gateway into Europe, and vice versa for them and similar Latin American conglomerates and investors.

'Lisker companies are principally established in the US, the Americas and the Far East, with total net income of more than US $350 million on total sales of more than $2 billion for their group. But the real interest for them is Europe. For Javier Lisker this is a personal quest.

'Their contacts in Brussels have shown them the initial concept and scope of the EEC project, its planned expansion and unification of currencies. Whenever such a project comes off, it will create a market equal or greater in size than the US. So being present in the EEC through Virtuvio makes all the sense in the world.'

Morales listened, enjoying the food. As far as he knew Lisker was a typical conglomerate, with interests in telecommunication equipment, food distribution, construction and finance. He also knew that it was Emilio de Ronin, the hard-charging chairman of the rapidly-expanding Banco del Norte y Cantabria, who had initially introduced Diaz to Lisker at a hunt on the de Ronin estate.

In contrast to others with similar large family companies, both Cantarini and Lisker kept very much to themselves. Unless you searched for them very specifically you wouldn't see them in the press. Their various companies and company structures – yes. But Cantarini had rarely been photographed, and Lisker very rarely. Javier Lisker seemed to appear only to sign contracts or smile and shake the hand of the other party. Otherwise he left no trail. Neither did he appear in Paris Match or Holà. And people who did business with him and did try to find out – understandably – who they were dealing with, got lost in a maze of holding companies, sub-holding companies, foundations and similar. Morales had tried to do this himself some time earlier, but with no tangible results. He made a mental note to start another full information check on Lisker.

Morales seemed to be satisfied.

'We'll sit down with your people to draft the press release of this deal you struck with Lisker and Cantarini, so we can really finalise the schedule of the IPO' he said. 'If it's OK with you we'll meet in London in two weeks to finalise all outstanding issues and to file the CNMV – the Spanish SEC – application for the IPO.'

'Of course' answered Cortes. 'And may we presume that with this solution on the table, as we promised to your bank, you will act as an underwriter to the issue?'

'A deal is a deal – you arranged for two external groups to support the Virtuvio business plan, so we will act as the lead underwriter for the share issue' answered Morales.

CHAPTER 7

'Which brings me to Project Clam' said Diaz. He had finished eating and lit a cigarette.

Project Clam was the name chosen for the study and execution of part of their post-IPO investment proceeds into BANINSA. When Morales and Rheinman had been made aware of their plans some four months previously they had immediately pitched to become the leading investment banker to the operation.

Divide and rule: Diaz and Cortes had logically anticipated this interest but had already discussed it with one of German's largest banks, Berlin Bank, who were also eager to expand into the growing Spanish market. Berlin Bank was also a lead underwriter in the Virtuvio flotation.

'We have identified, discussed with and made introductions with about 25% of Clam core shareholders, divided into roughly four groups' said Diaz. 'The premium these people expect is 10-15% over the quoted price. If we add to this what we have bought already directly and through third parties we would reach the 30% level. The free float is about 35% and relatively stable, so we should be able to take control within a reasonably short time scale.'

Plates were removed and coffee was served. Cortes lit one of his customary cigars.

Diaz continued: 'However, we have noticed that the trade in Clam shares has of late become more active than usual. We also were surprised to see RAM among the active buyers.' RAM was Rheinman Asset Management, one of Europe's fastest-growing asset management companies, 100% owned by Rheinman Partners.

Diaz paused and looked Morales straight in the eye. Coffee was brought in and Cortes lit a cigar. Morales made an attempt to answer, but Diaz kept going.

'Given Spain's attractiveness within the European context as a market for growth, this is understandable.'

Again Morales made an attempt to speak, but Diaz continued without looking at him.

'What did seem odd were a number of individual buyers, all of them offshore entities. It became clear after some investigating that they were privately-held investment vehicles, all of them sharing the same advisor and or administrative relation in one way or the other: RWME, in Zug, Switzerland.'

RWME stood for Rheinman Wealth Management Europe, the 100%-owned wealth management arm of Rheinman Partners.

Now Diaz looked Morales in the eye. 'So here we have, perhaps, a potential conflict of interest, Peter. Let me answer for you – no, neither you or your team of course mentioned anything to anybody. RWME and RAM share the same ownership but are separate units which take their own investment decisions. Still – what can we do about this?' He leaned back in his chair.

Morales started to answer, but Cortes took over from Diaz. He leaned forward, the cigar smoke of his Cohiba No. IV gently swirling around him, as if his face was framed in the smoke.

'Peter, let's cut to the chase. We can't have these share movements going on. It will undoubtedly lead to price increases, and that doesn't serve anybody's purpose. I presume you'll agree? Perhaps you and Rheinman didn't know, but we value very highly discretion by our own friends and allies, and above all those professionals who collaborate with us.'

Cortes, like Diaz, spoke very slowly, looking into Morales' eyes. His gaze had stopped many men. His light blue-grey eyes were set in a hawkish dark-skinned face. If you were smart, you paid attention. Pedro Cortes didn't say things twice. You either caught on immediately, or you should not have been part of the conversation.

Peter Morales was trained to pick up at the drop of a hat. A very direct message had been given to the Rheinman Partners representative. They were expected, as of this conversation, to stop 'front running'.

Front running was the unethical practice of a broker or adviser trading an equity based on information from the departments handling client orders before the client had been given the information. It was a well-established activity in Spain at that time.

Morales had had other conversations like this one with Cortes and Diaz. Now it was not a suggestion, it was an order. Only one answer was allowed.

'Of course, my personal apologies if any unfortunate actions were taken before consulting yourselves. And naturally I don't have any ideas or views regarding the activities of the two associated companies you mentioned. I am not in any position to comment on this. However, rest assured that immediately upon my return to London tomorrow I will discuss your concerns at group management level.'

Message received loud and clear.

Diaz had lit another cigarette. Cortes simply gazed at Morales while continuing to smoke his cigar and finish his glass of wine.

'Would you like another coffee?' Cortes asked. He spoke as if he had just asked Morales the name of his shoemaker.

On the pavement in front of the restaurant, Diaz and Cortes watched Morales get into his car and leave. Behind it appeared the Audi A8 for Diaz and Cortes, along with their security people who had been waiting near the restaurant. Diaz and Cortes got in, the security people hurried to their follow-up car and the two cars sped away.

The Guardia Civiles looking on from the entrances of the neighbouring buildings of the Ministry of Interior.

In the Audi, Diaz was on the phone to the head of the Project Clam team.

'Continue to screen buyers and sellers every day' he said. 'You were right, it was them. How did it close today?' He listened to the answer, covered the mouthpiece and looked at Cortes. 'It dropped a little, so let's buy more. OK?'

Cortes nodded.

'Buy tomorrow morning at opening through one of the UK-domiciled accounts we haven't used so far. I'll be back in 20 minutes.'

They had been actively screening through a large variety of sources to identify the movers and shakers with BANINSA stock. Diaz had been sure it was the Rheinman people. Both Diaz and Cortes had spent much time on getting to understand Rheinman and its business principals since the firm had been founded.

The other banks interested in Virtuvio were stock-exchange quoted companies – Rheinman had then been a closed partnership. Information was always available, but only when you used information gathered to act on it would value be produced.

After reading selected material on the firm, Diaz and Cortes had a very clear grasp of what made Rheinman so consistently successful, both at boom and bust stages of the economic cycle. Lately they had started to copy their investment banking leadership in the USA. Rheinman had stuck to one principle practically since the beginning. It took care to be leading on the three vectors of its business: to control the buyer, to control the seller and to be the only intermediate in the middle. A broker was another animal. Companies like Bear Stearns were brokers; Rheinman were intermediaries, thus controlling those three vectors as far as possible.

Another very simple and highly effective policy was to supply its biggest and brightest stars to its clients: to government, to regulatory market bodies, to the boards of its clients. Having to deal as a Rheinman banker with a President of the Board of a Fortune 500 company who was ex Rheinman tended to remove problems when pitching for one mandate or another.

Three working days later, all the financial press, led by the FT and the Wall Street Journal, reported on the last operation by the Virtuvio board in clinching two new international shareholders who were fully subscribing to the project. Two weeks later in London the underwriting consortium finalised it's documents to start its filing in Madrid with the CNMV. Less than six months later, Virtuvio was quoted on the Madrid stock exchange.

In parallel, and keeping in mind the revenues of the IPO from Virtuvio and their own holdings, Diaz and Cortes prepared for their final cornerstone investment – to become a shareholder of reference in one of Spain's leading and oldest banks, BANINSA.

Virtuvio had become an industrial conglomerate focusing on food and infrastructure-related industries. To have a large and important stake in a financial services corporation made all the sense in the world. In the months following the IPO, Diaz and Cortes were seeing and following closely the movements by the Spanish Central Bank, Banco de España, in orchestrating, together with the socialist government, the preparations for the Spanish financial system within the European market requirements.

The Minister of Finance, a socialist technician with a keen interest in preparing his own future and that of those close to his party, had an agenda in mind for doing this.

The government and the Minister didn't have any opposition to worry about - Spain was their own private hunting ground. No right-wing party had any real impact to politically oppose this, thanks to the burden of the Franco years.

And as any good politician knows, the game was always to survive four elected years, hopefully more, but always keeping in view their own economical future.

Being a minister was nice, but it didn't produce the income on its own. Turning power into income meant work. Being a socialist, wherever you were in Europe, meant eventually turning into a liberal and a controller of wealth, without being seen as one. In the end socialists were nothing more than fallen angels from the right who could do a deal with the devil, yet climb back to money and power.

This was Spain's third socialist government, and times were changing. The continuous stream of political scandals made any effective political governance a hopeless task. Voters, as always, had a tendency to get tired of their elected politicians after six years or so. Add to that the endless corruption and related scandals, and it meant that all government officials were closely watching their steps.

What better after a political career than joining the forces of money and commerce which you had supposedly been fighting on behalf of the poor voters? The banking system was the real hunting ground for such prizes. People and players in the banking system were also the ones who needed the most political favours.

Spanish banks, like German ones, were closely linked to industry and had large holdings in it, but none were big enough to compete outside Spain. Mergers and friendly takeovers had to be 'suggested' by the only body with a capacity to do so: the Banco de España.

Given that the Governor of the Banco de España was nominated by the Minister of Finance, all the ingredients were at hand, and under reasonable control.

This meant for Diaz and Cortes a pre-determined collision course.

Entering a Spanish bank as a new shareholder of reference meant direct scrutiny by the Banco de España. Long hours were taken by their analysts, trusted lawyers and advisors to come up with a strategy for how to get into a bank. Technically of course, the shares in a quoted company were free and tradeable, but in Spain at the time it didn't work that way. The political class and regional forces were on the alert for anybody trying to ease themselves in without a proper 'invitation'.

One German bank – Banco Berlin – had slipped in through a regional operation which couldn't be stopped. The Germans had been told that this must be their last unofficial movement of that kind. This message was laid down with the knowledge that Banco Berlin needed to grow further in Spain. But that was not going to happen any time soon after their quick putsch.

The BANINSA project consumed Ramon Diaz, and this greatly preoccupied Cortes. It also brought to light their main difference; Cortes was old money with an established family reputation and nothing to prove, while Diaz wanted to clinch exactly that elusive prize – the acknowledgement that he belonged to the same class as Cortes, but had got there in one generation.

This difference had worked for them when restructuring and formatting Virtuvio, but for Pedro Cortes life had moved on and different ventures abounded in a 'new' Spain. Cortes also knew that a lot of his old friends and friends-in-arms of the Spanish establishment were wary of his friendship with Diaz.

Diaz' ambition was eating him from within. Cortes wondered how long he would be able to contain himself.

CHAPTER 8

It was a bright October morning at the Castellana offices of Virtuvio, near the Villamagna hotel on Castellana. Diaz was softly whistling as he arrived.

'Hola Mari Carmen, esta Don Pedro?'

'He is waiting for you, please enter' answered Pedro Cortes' trusted secretary and personal assistant.

When Ramon entered Cortes' office it was the smell, as always, that caught him – a mixture of original Chesterfield chairs with 50-year-old leather, cleaned very delicately as they had belonged to Cortes' grandfather, and the lingering smell of Cuban cigars. The smell of power.

Pedro Cortes was dressed in the style he was known for, in a dark charcoal-grey double-breasted suit, made to measure by the same Madrid tailor who dressed King Juan Carlos I. A light blue shirt with a blue silk tie, no frills, no animals or other figures printed on it. His ties were made by an old woman in Rome whose address he shared with nobody. Finally, polished black tasselled loafers made by Crockett & Jones in London, the only people, according to Cortes, who understood what shoes were about.

In recent years Cortes had been had been wearing spectacles more and more often. This pair he had found at some shop in Athens, where the salesman had claimed that they had belonged originally to a well-known shipping magnate. Their effect was to make Cortes look like the late Aristotle Onassis.

Behind his very large writing desk was an enormous painting displaying Machiavelli in all his darkness. It caught most visitors off guard. The painting, its strategic location and the contrast with other more modern paintings in the room, always made people stop to think.

Cortes got up from his table and the men embraced.

'La familia bien? Kids OK?'

'Todo bien Pedro, graçias – I hope you will come to see them soon.'

'Bien lo haré. Let's sit.'

The two men moved to the sitting area in front of Cortes' writing table.

'Ramon, I need to talk to you about Virtuvio and how I would like to propose that we try to move on from here.'

Diaz crossed his legs. The conversation they were going to have had been cooking for some time. Pressure from within the Cortes family had been mounting on Pedro, but in keeping with his class and breeding he had said nothing. Friends were friends, business was business and family was family. In Spain that always proved to be the conclusive factor when dealing.

Diaz said nothing. Cortes went on: 'We have been very successful. I have gained a personal friendship which I couldn't have imagined at any previous time.'

Still silence.

'Your style of management and the economic results that have been achieved have been singular, but they are yours and yours alone.'

Diaz uncrossed his legs, about to make a comment.

'Please, let me finish' Cortes went on. 'Our relationship produced the setting and surroundings, but I know and feel that the time has come for me to leave it to you to continue with Virtuvio without me or the family surroundings that keep you at bay.'

Diaz watched Cortes' eyes. He knew this was a friend, someone who would never betray him. It was not in his nature.

'The time has come for each of us to go back to the freedom of action and style which started our venture. The time has come for the world to meet Ramon Diaz on his own terms. You deserve it.'

Cortes stopped, knowing that to say too much was to take away the impact of what he was saying.

'Also you know, I am not really a fan of getting into the newspapers every day.' He chuckled.

In fact it was Cortes' wife who had originated this last comment and Diaz knew it – she had never liked Diaz. Señora Cortes was old Spanish aristocracy dating back to the days of Felipe II. When a social upstart like Diaz was continuously in the headlines - much more than her own husband - she was bound to dislike him, whatever he did.

Diaz got up, maintaining eye contact with Cortes. He moved over to the window and its unique view over the Paseo de la Castellana. It was not that he hadn't expected this conversation to take place. He just never liked it when another party brought up delicate subjects. It was a question of being in control, and of being used to being in control. Nothing personal, as the Americans always put it.

A moment passed as Diaz formulated his answer. He turned towards the window.

'Pedro, let me begin by expressing my gratitude for your openness in voicing your point of view. We created this together and I always thought that we were going to end it together, wherever that is supposed to be.'

Diaz turned back from the window to face his business partner.

'Knowing you as I do, I will not prolong this into a long discussion about why we should continue our business relationship. Because knowing you, Pedro, this is something you have been thinking about for some time. Alone and with the pressure of your family.'

Cortes moved forward as if to reply, but directed his attention towards a large cigar humidor. He opened it and took out a Partagas

Siglo II cigar. Diaz waited as Cortes prepared his cigar, lit it and puffed out a curl of smoke.

'Without you Virtuvio doesn't make sense, Pedro. Not for me, not for the employees, not for the shareholders. But yes, if this is your wish then I will do my utmost to finish our project myself.'

A silence came over the room and the two business partners looked each other in the eye. Now it was out in the open.

An established Spanish family with more than sufficient funds had been catapulted into a new situation by making a pact with an extraordinarily intelligent caretaker, but their backgrounds were bound to clash eventually. Family companies and family owners of companies were extremely difficult and volatile entities to manage. In the long run, independent co-shareholders doubling as executive managers made for an unstable combination. And the difference in such an end situation derived from two very different kinds of intelligence. Very intelligent people will always come to a conclusion, whatever their background, because they know a solution must be found.

It was instinct which gave operators like Diaz and Cortes the ability to take a split-second decision. That was the difference between them and other capable and very intelligent business people – the drive to take a decision instead of delaying with endless deliberations, weighing the possibilities until the possibilities were not there any more. Now they faced the decision to separate their business interests.

The two business partners looked at each other, Cortes slowly enjoying his Partagas, Diaz waiting for his partner to react. Cortes looked up.

'Thanks for that. Let's decide how we go from here. I propose that we speak to KPMG for a fair value study and ask them to come up with a relatively easy execution strategy to separate our joint investments.

Regarding the BANINSA shares, I'll contact J P Morgan to place the block on the market. Let me get you the list I have.'

Cortes rose to his feet. Diaz listened, dumbfounded. This impersonal reaction had surprised him.

Half an hour after Diaz had left, Cortes was sitting in the back of his privately-owned Maserati Quattroporte. The car had been a present from his wife for his birthday in 1988, and he preferred it to the boring fleet of Audis and BMWs he had access to via the car pools of the various companies on whose boards he served. Nobody in the Madrid business community was surprised by Cortes and his black Maserati; it had become his trademark.

He turned in his seat and watched his security team's car vanish from view. He asked the security man sitting beside his driver for the phone. He dialled a number; it was answered at the third ring.

'Esta la señora…?'

A few moments later Cortes said to his wife: 'It's done. He agreed. I'll see you tonight.' He gave the phone back to the security man and leaned back in his seat.

Pedro Cortes y Ibarra, a friend of kings and queens everywhere he went, was the owner of one of Spain's most beautiful fincas, acknowledged as one of the most remarkable hunting estates in Europe. He was a man of enormous wealth, built by his family over centuries. Now he did not really know what he felt, but deep down he knew he was relieved. He felt the relief of someone who knew he had been very close to a great heat. That heat had been the all-consuming ambition of the man with whom he had shared an enormous adventure – Ramon Diaz.

The Maserati stopped at the traffic lights where Castellana met Maria de Molina. Cortes looked at the people crossing in front of the car. It was a typical crisp blue-sky day, with a sun which invited one to sit somewhere on a terrace.

Had he ever really known Diaz? Was he guilty in some way of keeping something back? That something was Diaz' ambition, an ambition for power fuelled by an ancient hunger by people with very high intelligence.

Diaz had searched over the years to equal Cortes in style, in personality, in everything. Cortes had had power since the day he had been born, while Diaz looked for, courted and fed upon it.

He shuddered in his seat at the conclusion which had led him to the meeting and settlement he had just come from – the knowledge that Ramon Diaz would be consumed by his own demons at some time and at some moment when he would not be expecting it.

Now the lights had changed and the Maserati and the security car accelerated away together.

Three weeks later, carefully orchestrated through top-notch Spanish PR companies, the market received the news that Pedro Cortes would leave his responsibilities at Virtuvio and its sister companies with immediate effect. In typical Madrid fashion, the news had already filtered through and was out on the streets, in the offices, the restaurants and the clubs, even the shooting events.

Ramon Diaz took out a major loan with Banco del Norte y Cantabria, guaranteed by the Virtuvio and other holdings. He also partially bought and swapped Virtuvio shares and cash in the Dutch BV for Pedro Cortes' stake. Ramon Diaz became the sole partner of the Cantarini and Lisker groups.

Over three weeks of marathon negotiations with bankers, brokers, lawyers, PR people, accountants, the CNMV (the Spanish equivalent of the SEC) to try to keep the process as short as possible, Diaz met several times through his own lawyers with the officers of Banco del Norte y Cantabria. As a result of these meetings, the size and impact of the loan he was soliciting proved greater than normal and very beneficial.

Diaz met with Juan de Ronin, prime member of the controlling shareholder family and CEO of Banco del Norte y Cantabria. De Ronin was a man even more used to having his ambitious way, which meant that any profitable operation in Spain should have his approval. The loan arrangement for Ramon Diaz was no different.

What Diaz didn't know was the unbelievable depth and strength of de Ronin's Banco del Norte y Cantabria network in South America. The Ronin family had for more than three generations slowly but surely extended their banking business there. South America was bound to fall under the influence of Spanish companies, so for the Ronin family this had been a clear path forward – follow your clients by leading them. This vision would come to full fruition in the decades to come.

This profound knowledge of Latin America became apparent to Diaz during his first lunch in Santander with de Ronin at the old HQ of Banco del Norte y Cantabria. Like many regional groups, they tended to have dual HQs.

The setting was the CEO's dining room and they were drinking coffee after a very sober lunch, typical of de Ronin - salad, grilled sardines, a glass of beer for de Ronin and one glass of white wine for Diaz. The waiters took away the plates and glasses and de Ronin began to explain his views about the South American continent, its individual markets and the risks in moving them.

'You are aware of the structure of your Colombian partners, the Lisker family?'

asked de Ronin suddenly.

'Yes – I know the Lisker family directly controls the 60% Colombian holding vehicle. Their activities in construction, distribution and banking are the principal part of their activities, originating from Brazil, Argentina, Mexico...' continued Diaz. He mentioned the publicly-known rates of return and profitability figures which he had been investigating since being introduced to them.

De Ronin looked fixedly at Diaz. His dark, piercing eyes were legendary in Spanish business circles. His ability to switch in one sentence from supportive and friendly to distant, cold and calculating were a trademark. When you worked for him or his family and Banco del Norte y Cantabria, it tended to be a short-term commitment.

Diaz finished at last.

'You have done a large part of your homework. What you didn't mention was any knowledge of the Lisker partners' 40% holding in the Colombian holding company, the one you will also partner with.'

Diaz said nothing. He waited for de Ronin to make his point.

'We at Banco del Norte y Cantabria did a true due-diligence review of all the Colombian vehicles, the partners involved, their backgrounds – everything. I have a warning for you. Perhaps you read some time ago that we planned to bid on the finance of a Colombian toll road. We initially teamed up with the Lisker family and their Colombian investment vehicle. We are under the supervision of the Banco de España, so we need to know who we are dealing with. And I want to know who I am dealing with.

'The Lisker part is not the problem: the activities are clear, where the money comes from etc, no problem at that end - as far as I have been able to conclude.'

He paused, looked at Diaz and took a sip of his coffee.

'Then we asked who the 40% partners really were. And we waited. No straight answers came forward, so I put this to Lisker. He said they would vouch for them and we said sorry, we need to know who they are ourselves. So we waited some more. Javier Lisker kept stalling, kept on presenting us with business people who were Consejeros and Board Members. But the real representatives for the Colombian vehicle's 40% proved to be a hard-nosed US lawyer based in Hamilton on the Bahamas.

'The only thing we found out was that the partners are – as far we could establish – clearly connected to a Bahamian bank which caters only for offshore clients. This bank doesn't solicit any other business, and neither is it open to anybody else to accommodate business.

'We could not ascertain who was what or who owned what in the Bahamian bank, so we, as Banco del Norte y Cantabria, had to withdraw from the financing of the toll road. Lisker accused us of not trusting him. We countered that only if we knew who was the end owner and could convey this to third parties like the Banco de España were we willing to proceed.

'After we cancelled our involvement, I personally asked the Harrilson agency to investigate further on my behalf, in view of other business relationships which we have with Lisker, controlled or directly-related vehicles throughout South America.'

Diaz didn't show it, but this comment hit home with Diaz. Nobody just 'used' the Harrilson organization, one of the foremost international forensic investigation agencies. You didn't use them just to understand the obvious but to map the risks of the hidden questions and resulting answers.

'After three months Harrilson resigned the assignment. They said two of their investigators had died in suspicious accidents, one in a car crash on a straight road – the driver had never drunk or driven too fast in his life – while the other was a drug overdose, and the victim was a woman who had never taken anything stronger than aspirin. One accident took place in Peru, the other in Colombia.

'Through local law enforcement agencies in both countries, Harrilson was advised not to pursue the matter further. That was when the CEO asked me to relieve them of the assignment.'

De Ronin's tone of voice had not changed throughout this speech, which gave it an even bigger impact.

'Diaz – Ramon - let me suggest to you that you keep a close watch on the Lisker partners.' He started to get up from his chair, and Diaz did likewise. De Ronin continued.

'When we reach agreement regarding your requested loan, a governing part of the loan agreement will carry the condition that if any problems should occur with the Lisker party or anybody related to them, the loan becomes payable within 10 days. This clause is at the sole discretion of Banco del Norte y Cantabria. I presume this is not a problem for you.'

Diaz didn't reply. He picked up his glass of water, drank some, got his lighter out of his jacket pocket and lit a cigarette.

'Thank you, Emilio, for sharing this information' he said. 'I will keep it in mind. And of course I do accept the clause regarding the Lisker party, so I will await the first draft of the loan agreement from your legal department.'

With this the meeting came to a close. Ramon Diaz now started his own investigations to find out who was behind the 40% stake of his partners in Colombia.

Virtuvio became a Ramon Diaz-guided vehicle when the buy-out of the Pedro Cortes family holding became a reality, financed by Emilio de Ronin and his bank.

From there on, business for Virtuvio continued to expand with Diaz and his management team producing excellent results, fuelled by European - and especially Spanish - economic growth. During those few years Diaz had nothing but smooth sailing with his partners Lisker and Cantarini.

CHAPTER 9

St Tropez, July 1983

Ramon Diaz' private plane, a dark blue Gulfstream bearing the BANINSA logo in red and gold, landed at the end of a typical sunny early July day morning at Le Môle, the small airport of St. Tropez, used almost exclusively for private aircraft.

The only other thing that mattered about the village of Le Môle was its main restaurant, in an old gas station, which seemed to be filled with people using the airport. Thanks to the affluence of its visitors, the restaurant had one of the best wine lists in the area, a well-kept secret.

Diaz, followed by his wife Yolanda and his two children, came down the steps of the Gulfstream and crossed over to where his car and security people were waiting. They had left Madrid the previous afternoon.

'Papa, where are we going?' asked his 10-year-old daughter Sophia for the umpteenth time since leaving Madrid. Five-year-old Julio was gripping his mother's hand and trying to wake up again after having fallen asleep on the flight.

'Didn't I promise we would be going to the beach?' said Diaz.

'Si Papa, pero cuando?'

'When we get there!' Diaz answered with a big smile. He was used to the constant questioning of his children.

The family got into the cars waiting on the tarmac; their luggage would be brought later. It was a 20-minute drive to the harbour of St Tropez. The traffic was manageable at that hour, at the beginning of July. The town, along with the rest of the South of France, was preparing itself for July and August, the time when the whole of Europe seemed to take their holidays there.

The harbour of St Tropez has three main features: its sights, its sounds and its smells. The sights are the large boats with their owners or hirers on the after decks, while the ordinary tourists stand, look on and eat junk food. The second layer of spectators sit in the cafeterias, bars like Senequier, Bar Le Port, Gorilla and the Hôtel Sube with its first floor terrace, giving the best view of the harbour and the Bay of St Tropez for drinks in the summer around seven o'clock. It marks the difference between a human bazaar and a painting done by nature, with ever-changing colours and light.

The sounds are mainly those of the powerboats, with their variety of engines ranging from the small Japanese outboards of the dinghies to the big V12 Lamborghini engines fitted to the offshore racers. Perhaps it is the only harbour where all the extremes of boat-users live together as one happy family.

The smell in July and August was one of diesel and gasoline fumes, lavender from the mountains, human sweat, French fries, and in the early morning, coffee and croissants.

This was the third year Diaz had kept his boat in the Gulf of Saint Tropez. He anchored it outside the harbour for security reasons. To keep it moored in the harbour during the summer was an invitation for the ever-present press and paparazzi to pester those on board. And the daily cost was outrageous for a boat the size of Diaz'.

From the quayside at the entrance to the harbour in front of the harbourmaster's office, two tenders transported Diaz and his family to the boat. The name of the boat was La Domada, The Wanderer, a reflection of his life and an easy choice. Seeing it and the hills surrounding the Bay of St. Tropez always cast a spell on Diaz. Perhaps it was the only place where he ever really relaxed.

La Domada was over 65 meters long and could sleep 10 people comfortably. It had a large permanent staff, year round. Diaz had bought the boat some time before from an English bank which had repossessed it from a distressed client. His financial problems had been so acute that he had never been able to use it. The transaction had been typical for Diaz; on a Monday in February, one of his lawyers in London mentioned to him that a client of the bank in question needed to sell the boat without it becoming public knowledge, which would drive the price down. Diaz and his people came to a verbal arrangement with the UK bank on the Tuesday, agreeing to buy it subject to certain technical issues and warranties by the shipyard, which of course also saw itself affected. These matters had been arranged on the Wednesday and Thursday and on the Friday before closing for business, Diaz had bought the boat at a discount of more than 55%, in cash. This was possible because the boat was in the name of an offshore company in the British Virgin Islands, so the share transaction was rapidly put in place by the bank and its distressed client.

Diaz now went to the Operations Room, dubbed by the Spanish-speaking sailors who manned the boat 'La Centralita', thanks to the huge amount of telecommunication equipment, which took care that Diaz or whoever needed it was in constant contact with whatever centre they needed to communicate with. The communication centre had been divided in two parts - a study and a connecting room with a personal assistant who managed all equipment.

Diaz went straight to his working table, picked up the phone, and punched in the mobile number of Javier Sanchez. As he waited for the connection, he started to scan the papers the assistant had left for his attention.

'Sanchez, can you hear me?'

'Si, Señor Presidente' came the reply, along with the typical interventions which seem standard when using portable phones in overcrowded European surroundings.

'Did they arrive?'

'Yes, all your guests are on their way and if all goes well the Americans should arrive tonight in Barcelona. We will pick them up there on our way to you in France.'

'OK, y hasta pronto.' Diaz hung up and sat back.

Everything was in place. When his guests signed the documents tomorrow, he would further consolidate his status as one of the youngest presidents of one of the main banks in Spain. The structure for the operation had been laid a year earlier, when Diaz had sold, together with his then partner Pedro Cortes, the shares of a part of the Virtuvio Group of companies to an Italian multinational. It concerned the sale of pharmaceutical companies, an area of industrial activity, both Diaz and Cortes agreed, which could only survive and grow either as a multinational or part of one. The cost of developing new medicine was almost exclusive to the multinationals and venture-capital sponsored initiatives.

Cortes always described it as like Formula 1 racing – the teams sponsored by the Ferraris, Fords and Mercedes of this world against private teams like Jordan and Williams, who either became successful and were then bought by the big names, or the money ran out and they disappeared. So when the Italians had approached them to open negotiations towards a possible sale, matters had moved swiftly. The personal windfall in the sale of Virtuvio's pharmaceutical companies made it possible for Diaz to renegotiate terms and conditions with de Ronin and his Banco del Norte y Cantabria.

Diaz finished reading the various papers, gave instructions to his assistant, got up and went below, stopping now and then to salute sailors and other staff on board. When he got down to the boat's bodega level, the sailors were busy preparing the winches to place a gleaming dark blue object on to the quay. They had to navigate carefully between tenders, rowing dinghies, waterskis and other objects which were tied and secured in this area of the boat. As the object settled on the quay, an ever-increasing number of passers-by stopped to look. It was Diaz' gleaming silver and blue 1959 Harley Davidson.

Diaz was about to do what he always particularly enjoyed doing during his stays in the South of France – take his beloved machine for a spin around the hills of Ramatuelle and through the back roads to St Tropez.

He left the bodega and climbed on to the quay. The Harley roared into life, and the rumbling sound of its engine filled the space between La Domada and the crowd of onlookers.

'Papa! PAPA!'

It was his daughter Sophia calling from the upper part of the boat. She always wanted to go along with him on such little outing around the neighbourhood of St Tropez and beyond.

Like all daughters, Sophia was a copy of her father - not only the way she was built but in her reactions. Ten-year-old girls are sharp and observant. Sophia loved anything to do with speed. She read adult books, read the Financial Times with her mother at least once a week and was always interested in learning anything new or meeting somebody new.

'Papa – espera voy contigo!' I want to go with you!

Diaz revved the engine and made as if to ride away. But there was a wide smile on his face. Sophia climbed in a flash down from the second deck, using parts of the hull even the sailors hadn't thought of, and settled on the back of the Harley. The sailors, most of them Spaniards and South Americans, had been screened and hand picked by

Virtuvio's security department. They always enjoyed the presence of Diaz' children as they were extremely well behaved and disciplined, yet shared a great sense of humour.

'Anda guapa! Andale, andale!' Go on, beautiful!

To a chorus of shouts and jeers from La Domada, Diaz slowly pulled through the crowds, revving the engine of the Harley. He passed La Gorille with its mainly French crowd, turned sharply right and right again and headed for the exit for Ramatuelle. Once outside the town, he made sure Sophia was still holding him firmly before slowly increasing speed.

The road from St Tropez to Ramatuelle – the Route de la Plage – was relatively quiet for the season and the time of day, but with a fair number of cars and small bikes as always. The pastel colours you see only in an early summer in Provence whizzed by – greens and browns, mixed with the azure reflection of the sea nearby, the light browns and pinks of the houses.

After a few kilometres, Diaz turned left. A few more minutes and he was cutting the engine on a parking space near the Nioulargue, one of the beach restaurants where Diaz and his family had lunch almost twice a week when they were not cruising on La Domada to other places near these Pampelonne beaches.

The Nioulargue was by far the most family-minded of the Ramatuelle beach restaurants. The Diaz family and friends had tried them all. Club 55 was voted too snobby and too much for rich tourists. La Voile Rouge had drugs and the shouting of horny English investment bankers. Tahiti was for Easter and Christmas.

'Bonjour M. Diaz. Comment ça va? La famille? Como estas, Sophia?'

Didier, the maître, immediately came towards Diaz as he entered. Sophia was already starting to head for the beach part, but first she gave him a polite kiss and answered Didier in French.

'Merci, en forme' answered Diaz as he walked towards the bar which bordered the private area. He ordered a still water with two wedges of lemon and no ice and sat down on one of the lounge chairs. The sea was still, azure and not too polluted. It would be some hours before the beach would fill with boats of all types and sizes. From lunchtime onwards, the pitch and sound of engines from the sea would increase.

Sophia had already taken off her shorts and shirt and was in the sea before her father could say anything.

Diaz smiled and leaned back. His phone went off - his wife Yolanda calling from the boat.

'Glad you helped with the suitcases.' She spoke slowly.

'I don't want to disturb people who are far better qualified for that sort of thing!' laughed Diaz.

'Que plan hay? Tu hija ya esta nadando?' Your daughter's gone swimming already?

'The plan is I will be back to pick up the two of you at the boat, I'll do the shopping you need and lunch on the beach. And yes, your daughter has gone for a swim. No permission asked of course. I'll find a towel somewhere to dry her before heading back.'

'Sabes que te queiro mucho, Señor Diaz?' I love you very much.

'Mismo digo y para siempre. Me too, always. How is Junior?'

'He's angry that Sophia always seems to have the best part of the fun when her father is around.'

'Tell him to grow up faster and become a girl, and that way he'll strike the same deals as his sister' answered Diaz.

'Oh yes, there was a call from Madrid. The people you are waiting for will be coming to the boat for drinks at the agreed hour, no delays.'

'Gracias mi señora, te veo pronto' said Diaz, and rang off.

Diaz shared only part of his professional life with his wife. She knew instinctively when to probe or cajole and when to stop. This was not out of any lack of trust or lack of intelligence - Yolanda Ruiz de la Arca, second daughter of the Marquesa de Trujillos de Sainz, had been a businesswoman in her own right before she had married, against the wishes of her mother.

Yolanda's father Ramon had been a man of vision who had prospered in the Spain of Franco through hard work and one basic idea – a strong enough foundation to form a basis for international expansion. By the time incurable cancer had ended his life at 46, he had become one of Spain's most successful international businessmen. Carla, his wife and the mother of Yolanda and his other five children, had done something which was not expected in those days; she had continued the work of her husband, developing his business and their dream.

Yolanda had been trained in the Trujillos family business with an iron hand by her mother. The textile business was an ever-evolving concept, with products never going out of fashion but following the fashion trends. To support their ever-growing chain of shops, the Trujillos were among the first to have their garments produced in Morocco, Turkey and the Far East.

After Ramon's death Yolanda's mother had a passionate love affair with an Englishman in Hong Kong, and started making garments there and in China. They were then shipped to Macau, which belonged to Portugal, and came into Spain via Portugal, thus cutting import duties to practically nothing.

School, university and the family firm had therefore been drilled into Yolanda from very early on. Any free time was used for on-the-job training by Yolanda's mother, involving one of their business relationships somewhere in the world.

Carla knew one thing for sure: if you taught a child business as part of play, it would become a natural process. Otherwise the child would get bored and rebellious and develop a natural aversion to everything associated with the family business.

When Diaz met Yolanda in New York for the first time, she was working at the mammoth Sears group as an apprentice in the fashion acquisition department. Love struck between the 24-year-old Diaz and 21-year-old Yolanda at the Rockefeller Centre skating rink, the mighty Christmas tree throwing a warm glow on to their handsome Spanish faces in the December cold of New York.

Diaz was then working at the law offices of Spitz & Whitman, thanks to a thesis which had piqued the interest of one of the senior partners at the Madrid firm of Tomas Menendes de Vigo, who had great belief in the future of a Diaz at their firm. He had met Yolanda's mother for the first time for lunch at the Plaza Hotel's oyster bar two months later, when New York was still locked in a deep winter frost. Carla was full of courtesy, but her manner was as icy as the exterior of the Plaza's restaurant. In the eyes of his future mother-in-law Diaz came from a different social class, and that was that. No power, money or superior intelligence could change it.

Diaz sensed this from the beginning when courting Yolanda, but he wisely never tried to confront the issue with Carla. He had one thing in mind and one only: Yolanda was going to be his wife.

He always described to his friends it as a situation similar to the Jews and Arabs in Palestine – neither of them was going anywhere. Once they were resigned to it, as Diaz said, the second and third generations would inevitably start to relate to one another. The relationship with Yolanda's mother Carla would always be civilized, but distant.

Diaz was a lone wolf in his business dealings, and he shared with Yolanda only what he wanted to share. The rest of their relationship was as rock solid and centred on each other, their children and a continuous battle to win Diaz' time, given his working habits.

Carla and Diaz never became friends, but Carla could not help seeing that Ramon Diaz had made her daughter a very happy wife and mother.

Sophia continued to play by the sea with the single-minded concentration only children have. They stayed for another 30 minutes before Diaz was persuaded to lunch on sushi, and drove back to St Tropez over the Route de la Plage. The rest of the day was spent between lunch, a stroll through the back streets of the harbour and Diaz catching up on reading files which he had brought with him on the plane from Madrid.

The next day, over a family lunch, they decided to go out in the boat.

CHAPTER 10

The next day, some time before French dinner time (or drinks time, for any Spanish or other Latin entourage), on the upper deck of La Domada, Diaz sat down with Felipe Lisker, patriarch of the Lisker empire and the third Lisker to head an originally Columbian dynasty of coffee growers who now lived between houses in Bogotà Miami, New York and London and also covered metal trading and a construction and food distribution empire as well as the original coffee business.

Lisker was dressed in St Tropez style – casual light blue cotton pants, a shirt emblazoned with the Cigarette powerboat brand and light brown Tods, never socks. The heavy gold chain around his neck was a further sign of laid-back wealth.

Given that he was always well tanned, his thin Mestizo face with a healthy mop of jet black hair streaked with a grey twist made him more the typical Côte d'Azur local than a business tycoon. It was an exotic mixture with an enormous appeal for women, which ensured that marriage had never been something he had contemplated.

The other guest, Giancarlo Cantarini, was still finalising some epic battles at the backgammon board with the Diaz children, amid a fair amount of shrieking and banter. The firm of Cantarini, similar to Lisker in its Latin America background, was an old and established Milan family powerhouse and one of the clear leading factors within the so called the Saloto Buono, the configuration of anything that meant real power in Italy from the days of the founders of Mediobanca, Italy's leading investment bank house and the likes of the Agnellis and Benettons. Power, politics, changes in industry, dividing influence - everything went through the hands, ears and minds of the Saloto Buono for the good of themselves and of Italy, whichever was more important for the situation in hand.

Giancarlo Cantarini was an extremely handsome and intelligent man of about 48 years old. He had the looks and build of a young Cary Grant, even wearing the same glasses. In contrast to Lisker, Cantarini had been happily married for more than 20 years to the daughter of one of the individual majority shareholders in Mediobanca.

Like Lisker, they seemed to have been born and bred for the jobs their families had reared and trained them for – keeping the wealth in the family and growing it into something stronger and more powerful on their watch as leaders of their houses. The two of them had shared more operations during the last five years: a cement factory in Germany and a portfolio of oil refineries in Turkey among others.

All these deals had been sourced by Broncecave, which took care of structuring them and finding external financial partners and bank finance, so that when the Spain situation with Virtuvio's IPO developed into plans for an assault on BANINSA it was more than logical that Lisker and Cantarini should become familiar with Diaz and Cortez.

Felipe Lisker had sat down beside Diaz, whose chair was turned so that he could have a unique view of the Bay of St Tropez with the sun setting, the sounds of the harbour changing from day to nightlife and the last boats coming into the harbour after a day on the water.

'Puro?' asked Diaz.

'Gracias – but after dinner' answered Lisker.

'How are they doing? Any indication how the placement is going?' asked Lisker, referring to Broncecave and the documents spread beside Diaz' chair.

Diaz looked at his wife and children moving away from the top deck to leave the men to enjoy a pre-dinner drink and dinner on their own.

'The placement has been going well since the end of the roadshow last week' he said. 'About 75% have been pre-placed by them and they expect it to be over-subscribed four to five times by the institutional investors outside Spain. For the Spanish market we are now at 95% for the institutional tranche and over-subscribed almost five times for the private market. They'll come back within the next week to indicate if they want to issue more shares or if they'll increase further the issue price.'

Lisker smiled. He already knew these figures through his own contacts at Broncecave management level.

'Good stuff Ramon, then we can celebrate the signature on the deal tonight' Lisker exclaimed.

'Plus some dancing at the Byblos' added Cantarini.

'Eres muy viejo para eso!' laughed Diaz, who always went a few times to one of St Tropez' most famous discotheques alone with his wife, just to celebrate a night out, no kids.

Diaz called to his personal assistant to bring the other documents which had been prepared over the past few weeks, which detailed the holding vehicle in Holland for the 55% shareholding of the three partners in Virtuvio. Then dinner was called.

Towards the end of dinner and with coffee and cigars served, Lisker's phone rang. He looked to see who was calling, got up and moved to the front of the boat to take the call in privacy.

'Si?'

'Patron, Bahamas called - the lawyer from New York died' answered a familiar Spanish voice.

'So? He was old. What has that go to do with us?'

'When we last went through his stuff, we found that he was building some kind of file which we reported on.'

Lisker staff kept close tabs on a number of people who were closely involved with Lisker, his business and his family. This surveillance included any kind of intelligence, sometimes legal but in most cases illegal; it included breaking and entering offices, tapping phone lines, hacking into computers, following people and photographing them. Anything to have everything ready in case people didn't follow Lisker's 'suggestions' and reasonable 'requests'.

The lawyer from New York had been running the international side of the Lisker family holdings for more than 15 years and was more than aware of the real origins of Lisker and his family fortune.

'When was the last time we checked this?'

'More than two months ago, Patron.'

'I'll come back to you.'

'Si, Patron.'

Lisker clicked off and looked out over the dark St Tropez harbour in the direction of Saint Maxime and the reflection of lights of the other villages like Gassin and Port Grimaud bordering the gulf. He immediately felt it, he didn't know why or how, but he was seldom mistaken. It was a hunch, a sixth sense – something that had protected him on a number of occasions. A feeling that something bad was going to happen.

He had tried to analyse it but couldn't come up with a rational explanation. Even so he always followed these feelings, these, thoughts these flashes.

A problem was brewing, and it had been brewing for more than two months, ever since his people had discovered a routine break-in on the personal PC of the New York lawyer, Lenny Gerstner.

People like Lisker had that special sense of smell or feeling which kept them alive. They were always alert for situations which other people only noticed at a later stage, when it was far too late.

It had been 20 years since Lisker had made that vital step from a previous life as one of Colombia's largest drug dealers, in the shadow of groups like the Cali cartel, Pablo Escobar, Carlos Lehder and other Medellin-related traffickers. There was a difference between 'them', as he called them, and him.

Lisker had got into the drugs business for one basic reason. Money.

Being a fourth-generation coffee grower – a fairly large one at that – was not enough for Felipe Lisker. It never had been. He had sometimes laughed when he explained to his partners in the drugs business that there was no special, heart-breaking story about it. It was just the step from a structured honest business world to trading in cocaine.

Just for the money.

Simple - cocaine was far more profitable than coffee could ever be.

And there was something else, equally unromantic: the Lisker family's vast Colombian fincas near the Brazilian and Peruvian borders were in the middle of nowhere, near the Caqueta river and the region around La Libertad. For more than 50 years the farmers had been openly growing coca plants on their small plots when not working the coffee fields of the Lisker family. Mainly for their own consumption, but it naturally grew into a decent side business in combination with the income the Lisker coffee activities brought to those farming families.

First, on a small scale, the coca crop was sold to local dealers and traffickers, a side business which became bigger as its profits became bigger. These were the years when people like Escobar and the others had started their meteoric rise in the drugs business. During those first years, and before the US Colombian treaty on their War on Drugs, the extraditions of drug dealers to the US, the drugs trade hadn't involved any violence. The various clans involved each had their areas and parts they worked at. Operational and organizational matters were to be shared. Matters were to be discussed and settled. It was a cottage business which was bound to take off.

Curiously, it was Escobar who pushed for joining forces.

Like any piece of history, the beginning was nothing to write home about. The drugs trade proved to be no different – a combination of smart, poor and entrepreneurial people started the trade. It wasn't legal, but neither was it really illegal. It was acceptable for those times. The coffee crop didn't perform for natural reasons - drought, crop diseases, or market reasons. Drugs – especially cocaine – were another matter.

That is until a Brazilian, Ramon Soza, came by one day to pay a visit to Felipe's father. Soza already had a small but stable business relationship with Lisker senior, and at certain times he bought coffee from him and traded with a number of large Brazilian distribution companies. But there was one thing Felipe's father didn't know about him -that 'Loco' Soza was Brazil's greatest undercover drug dealer.

Felipe's father knew only about Soza's legal business – coffee and rubber trading. To him, Soza was a friendly small-time Brazilian contact who didn't have any further bearing on his world. And what Felipe's father had never caught on to was the incredible level of intelligence Soza had – because he had been studying very patiently the Lisker set-up, the coffee business, the relationship between Lisker father and son.

Soza, like many very successful people, was extremely patient in working towards a goal, but very quick and ruthless if the goal or the game changed. And Ramon Soza became involved in drugs initially as a side business; friends asked him to 'transport' certain packages alongside his international coffee shipments. They paid too handsomely for such basic transportation services. It didn't take Soza very long to figure this out. Mutual business success is always a strong binding element for the breakdown of financial greed.

So Soza kept the coffee and rubber business growing nicely, but kept it out of the limelight. His distribution control became stronger and stronger for those having to ship increasingly their prime merchandise – drugs. For mutual interest of course, Soza built up his network of distribution as far as the US frontiers, carefully building himself a name as, first and foremost, a reliable shipper.

Having realised that his friends' businesses were bringing wealth in unheard-of volumes, he asked himself - why not join them, instead of just being a trafficker with a relative high risk profile, compared with the producers and fixers in the middle? When Ramon Soza really branched out into drugs – cocaine mainly– his business eye and acumen quickly made him look out for deserted areas near the borders of Brazil, Colombia and Peru where he could pack his merchandise and transport it to the largest and fastest-growing market – the United States.

Then into the picture came Lisker senior, the location of the Lisker fincas and their established, though small, coffee trade. It didn't take long for the patient Soza to find out that the younger Lisker wanted something different in life from his father.

Money.

So during his visits to Lisker senior over the years, he started to cultivate his relationship with young Felipe, then in his early thirties. Naturally, after a prudent period of time, when Felipe was on one of his trips to São Paulo to discuss coffee with Soza, he received a direct approach from him. Soza was a likeable guy, especially when building up his relationships, and he knew how to 'read' people. For him, the young son of old Lisker was an easy target. He sensed early on that Felipe valued only one thing. The coffee trade, the estate, the relationships, the history; these were only means to Felipe his single ambition in life, to make money.

Soza's proposal was simple. The Lisker estate was already selling a quantity of coca leaves to third parties. He knew this through talking to the farmers on the estate while discussing the coffee bean crops. He explained to Felipe that the cocaine and assorted businesses had come of age, and these third parties really made the money. He sketched it out on a small piece of paper at the dinner table during one of their first encounters without Felipe's father present. From raw coca leaves to consumable cocaine, ready to be inhaled, injected or whatever people liked, or could invent.

Soza and his organisation had the chemicals, the production and the storage facilities near the borders with Colombia. Most important of all, they had the connections and means to ship the product to the largest market, the USA.

Why not team up together, Soza proposed? The raw product was already there, but they would jointly invest some money in the production side and build a number of small laboratories on the vast Lisker estate. Soza would take care of the rest once these laboratories delivered the finished product.

They made some further calculations at the dinner table that memorable night. The figures astounded Felipe Lisker. Combining the coca business with the established coffee trade would bring him the wealth he had been dreaming of since he had left university and joined the family business.

At the end of their dinner, Felipe asked to be given a few weeks to come back to Soza with a final answer. He didn't need the time to settle his scruples or his conscious - he needed it to find out how handle this resulting increase in the cocaine business without getting into a fight with his father.

It was one thing for the local workers dabbling in a little coca leaf trade on the side, but a full-blown cocaine trade run by Felipe would result in an unavoidable clash between father and son. If only from the point of sheer decency – the father instilled within him the values of a decent human being and a businessman at the head of a family company. Actively soliciting a criminal activity was different – there was no room for that.

Felipe was ambivalent towards his father, but one thing he did have very clear in his mind – he was not going to end up as a reasonably wealthy and respected coffee grower in some lost corner of South America. Felipe's burning ambition was to be seriously wealthy, with no rules. For him it was clear that he who had real wealth wrote his own rules. Punto y pelota – that was the phrase his Spanish cousins had taught him. Game over.

All these years later, Felipe still kept the little note Soza had made that night with their first calculations. In fact the real wealth created through their mutual drugs dealing had beaten his calculations many times over.

They met again about three weeks later, at the same restaurant in São Paulo. Lisker had made up his mind. He had only two conditions: the venture should be on a 50/50 basis and his involvement must be kept totally secret, so there would be no direct links between them. This meant severing their present coffee trading relationship. Soza immediately agreed to both points.

This was the end of the 1970s and the beginning of the 1980s, and the drugs trade was picking up in speed, size and profitability. It was attracting increasing attention from new entrants and from law enforcement and there was a need to structure the income streams from the trade. It was this last point that drew Felipe Lisker to Soza. Soza was way before his time, far ahead of the boom the drugs business was about to go through.

CHAPTER 11

Soza explained during their various meetings over the years how he saw the future - the size and speed of the change to come to the drugs trade. He knew that in such a highly lucrative but dangerous business the place to be was in the shadows. But he explained his one and only rule: the drugs trade was a business, and it should be ruled, organised and run as a business.

It was of course a business in which violence was a risk factor. That violence had to be separated and contained as much as possible. It attracted 'attention'. And attention, as Soza explained, doesn't produce income - only cost. Personal security, transport security, lawyers, bribes, protection money - all such related items carried 'attention' with them.

The timing of Felipe's approach was perfect. Lisker senior was already planning to hand over the family business to him, evading any unsavoury family confrontation between father and son over the fact that the son was planning to plunge the family business into the drugs trade. So when father and son prepared the way for Felipe to take over the family business, it had been his late father who had unwittingly introduced Felipe to a vital component in his scheme.

Somebody was needed to be the intellectual architect for a scheme to hide the enormous growth of sudden extra income and wealth Felipe Lisker would experience after joining forces with Soza.

As with any growing business, structures were needed and bogus companies had to be set up to take care of the stream of income the Lisker and Soza venture was starting to generate. They had started with lawyers in Bogotà and São Paulo, who had introduced them to others in Panama and Curaçao, but the pace of the business was outgrowing such advisors.

Lisker wanted to shift more and more of his wealth to the US and beyond, but lacked the contacts to help him at this initial stage. It was not going to be a case of taking a plane to New York or Miami, having a few meetings with law firms and explaining to them that they would like advice about reinvesting drugs money in the US system. They needed a special somebody to help them structure their business future.

That somebody was to be Lenny Gerstner.

As usual in business life, the meeting which began the ongoing relationship was a casual one. Around the beginning of the eighties, Lisker senior was asked by the then vice president of Colombia's Central Bank to come to Bogotà for a lunch meeting to meet a respected lawyer from New York at the house of the US Ambassador. Lisker senior didn't very much like Americans, although he had had business dealings with them for years. He liked meeting and socialising with those who worked in or with his government even less. However the Central Bank's Vice President was an old school friend of Felipe's father since his schooldays, and a favour to a friend was always granted. He took Felipe with him.

The lunch at the US Ambassador's compound proved different things for father and son. The lunch showed that Lenny Gerstner was a high-calibre professional in his field. Felipe's father was not really into the conversation and spent most of the time chatting with his friend, the Central Bank's Vice President, and the Ambassador, but Felipe instantly had rapport with Gerstner.

Gerstner, like any American, quickly came to the point at the end of the lunch once he and Felipe were sitting alone on the porch drinking coffee with brandy and smoking some Cohibas which Felipe had brought along, not trusting the mediocre Dominican cigars offered by the Ambassador. As Felipe had been taught by an Englishman – a member of the Duke of Westminster's family - during his university days, Cuban cigars were like Ferraris – the top-of-the-line brand, leaving all others as imitations.

Gerstner's point was that he worked for certain US companies, directly enlisted by the US Government in matters related to security, and that his clients were looking for vast pieces of land to build training facilities. No names were mentioned, only that the companies mainly came from the southern part of the USA. Their identities were easy to guess for anybody like Lisker with an extensive knowledge of international business.

Already it was well known to informed South Americans that the CIA was all over their continent, trying to build up as much intelligence power as possible, in whatever form and disguise, to maintain a regional influence. Nicaragua had been a wake-up call in the usual US Government failure to understand what people want. Not the Somoza type of dictator, for sure.

Years later, Felipe remembered looking straight at Gerstner's face and saying:

'So Mr Gerstner, the State Department, or the CIA, or some other branch of your US Government is looking for isolated, well-connected terrains to train troops and engage in counter intelligence in bordering countries?'

Lisker's directness didn't surprise Gerstner. The information he had been handed before lunch on both Liskers was clear: US and other international education, astute international business people, independently wealthy through coffee and land holdings and related for generations to Colombian élite families. These same sources said that the son was taking over and that he seemed to have been getting wealthier, faster, than his father for the past two years, since taking over the managerial reins. Drugs trafficking was suspected but so far not proven, according to these sources. They had recommended that he focus on the son.

'Would that bother you?' Gerstner answered.

'Depends.'

'On what?'

'What it is you and your government want exactly. To rent some of our terrains, however remote they may be, and to start private wars on someone else's behalf is not something my father and I would want to be part of. Not even for your government.'

Felipe blew smoke from his cigar and sat back. Gerstner waited a few moments, pulled on his own cigar and took a sip of Spanish brandy.

'My clients would reward your cooperation in a very substantial way' he said. 'They would be willing to be instrumental in any Lisker professional activity to be run from US territory, now and in the foreseeable future.'

'The foreseeable future? Sorry, but I don't understand this exactly. You mean during the present legislation of your president?'

'My clients are not strictly bound by the political climate of a certain period. They have a more institutional view for the medium to long term for the interest they serve' answered Gerstner.

Felipe looked out over the gardens of the US Ambassador's compound, thinking.

'Mr Gerstner, let us ask, if in principal my family and I were interested in pursuing this conversation further, what would be first of your clients' needs?'

Gerstner turned his head. An aide brought over his Hartmann business case, opened it and spread out a map on the table between them. He pointed at the area near the Caqueta river and the region around La Libertad, circling it with a well-manicured middle finger.

'This area of 160,500 square kilometers is situated in the border area between Peru and Colombia, in the Amazon Basin. Its estimated population in 1985 was 96,800 inhabitants, of which Indians comprise about 16%. The specific area of interest for my clients is near Putumayo and Puerto Leguizamo, and forms part of your finca Los Carrizos, we understand. The interest of my clients would be an area of roughly 150 hectares at the very edge, not occupying any arable land or with any people living on it.

'My clients would build only very simple living quarters for about 40 to 50 permanent workers. Guards would be put in place. My client would like to build an airstrip for small to medium-sized aircraft.'

Lisker looked up with a frown. Airstrips were for the military, and the military-run government.

'We have already taken the liberty of discussing this specific necessity with your government and have already received their written approval' Gerstner continued.

He took another file from the attaché case and handed it to Lisker. The paper was an original, with a government seal and letter heading, and it was from the Colombian Minister of Defence to Gerstner's law firm in New York as the legal representatives for a Bahamian trust company called Mercado Libre Ltd. It was dated one month earlier and referred to a series of meetings and approved documents and ended with the formal authorisation of the construction of an airstrip and auxiliary structures and other relevant details, standard for such authorisations. Of course no real details or specific locations were mentioned.

One receiving government and its responsible officials were being flexible with another contributing government's request, thought Lisker. He got up, walked towards the end of the porch and looked out over the spectacular garden with its ornamental pond. The crickets of the Colombian jungle were giving their nightly concert, and it seemed louder and more urgent than ever. He knew this was the moment to implement the most difficult part of his personal plan, but it was also a unique opportunity - to be a producer of dangerous drugs yet be free to go into the business as if it was fully legitimate and approved by your biggest client - the US market and its government.

By the time he had turned round and walked back to Gerstner, who was sitting quietly waiting and smoking his cigar, Lisker had made up his mind.

'Mr Gerstner, let's do the following. I'll discuss this with my father and if he agrees, I'll instruct our lawyers to contact you directly to proceed with the final planning for this transaction.'

'Thank you Mr Lisker' said Gerstner. 'I will await your reaction accordingly.' He got to his feet. What a hungry young man you are, Mr Lisker junior, he thought as he shook Felipe's hand.

CHAPTER 12

Felipe's father died suddenly a few weeks later peacefully in his sleep after a massive coronary attack, as the doctor's autopsy later concluded. Father and son were spared the inter-generational discussions about the handing over of the business, and especially the fundamental issues of basic principle, which Lisker senior had known his son entirely lacked. So Felipe Lisker the Fourth was suddenly free to pursue his dream.

As a first step he made a very generous offer to his three older sisters. All of them were married to wealthy husbands, living with their families respectively in Bogotà, Miami and Santo Domingo. They had never liked the coffee business and were very happy over time that their only brother had gone into it, thus fulfilling the family tradition and ensuring they received an annual dividend.

Two months later, a Bahamian company called Mercado Libre Ltd effectively leased 250 hectares of land from the Lisker estate for a fixed 25-year period, renewable for additional 10-year periods. The whole of the transaction was typically done with a speed that is impossible in Colombia unless the government is directly involved.

Apart from the unrealistic price paid for the lease of the lands, Lisker had proved to be a hard bargain for Gerstner and his clients. The deal in the end was decided as a 25-year lease with an option either to renew or for Lisker to reclaim the land by paying a fixed amount for the construction done, the airstrip and similar. Of course, Gerstner offered Lisker the services of his firm to do the paperwork, and Lisker accepted happily.

As an extra condition, Lisker was allowed to use the airstrip for transporting any goods he wanted to ship from Los Carrizos.

In addition, as a sign of the power of Gerstner's client, Lisker and his family were to be given permanent non-dated US identity papers, making them part of the army of New York's United Nations officials from US friendly governments. This way there would be no hassles, no personal border or customs questions when arriving or departing for anywhere in the US.

It was diplomatic immunity in a very practical format. When Lisker explained the set-up to Ramon Soza, he whooped for joy. Their venture could not possibly have got off to a better start.

In less than eight months, the land was cleared and the airstrip constructed. From then on, a steady stream of cargo planes arrived. Most of them, according to those watching it day and night for Lisker and Soza, arrived with no identification at all or were Colombian military craft, reflecting the direct ongoing involvement of the government, or at least somebody very closely linked to it.

The people manning this strip were a mixture of Americans, Mexicans, Brazilians and other Spanish speakers of South American extraction, all with very obvious military bearing. The buildings which housed them were clearly barracks, with security perimeters swiftly put in place, protected by state of-the-art surveillance electronics.

Lisker had met through Gerstner's New York office with a Mr Smith, the permanent representative of Mercado Libre Ltd. in Colombia, who effectively had lived at the site from the moment the contracts of the deal had been signed. Mr Smith would be a permanent fixture as far as Lisker was concerned when requesting the use of the airstrip.

If Mr Smith - if that was his real name – was ever aware of the transport going out from Los Carrizos, he never showed that he cared about it. As he said soon after he had arrived 'Señor Lisker, I understand that you are in the production and export of high-quality coffee and have been authorised to use our facilities when technically available. That is all I need to know.'

In the meantime, Soza and Lisker had built their first laboratories at a safe distance from the strip and Soza had taken care that cocaine production rapidly came on stream. Within six months the Soza and Lisker operation was flying cocaine to Mexico and than onwards to the USA. From that moment, Lisker began to make frequent visits to New York and Los Angeles to structure the operation for investing the money he was making in the venture. For obvious reasons he had also left Colombia and used Lima instead as his base when he was in the area.

He also had made a very clear deal with Soza – they were together in the production side of the venture but on the revenue stream coming from it, they were to be completely separate. Soza didn't have a problem with this; it made sense to diversify away from one's partners.

What Soza didn't know was that it all formed part of Lisker's plan to walk away as soon as his profits had been recycled in sufficient diversified legal businesses, and when the ever-growing international drug enforcement forces had reached such a level that the risks were too big to keep their production and shipping venture alive.

These were the thoughts that were going through the head of Felipe Lisker as he took the phone call on Diaz' boat in the harbour of St Tropez.

It had been Lisker who had come up with the name of their joint initiative to support and invest alongside Ramon Diaz in the Virtuvio IPO – Pacto Contreras.

When the Virtuvio operation was signed, he gave them all an engraved golden Dupont lighter. Just like the one with which he now re-lit his Cohiba cigar.

The venture with Soza had proved hugely profitable. It had stayed clear where Pablo Escobar's had gone so badly wrong – too big, too loud and with too much violence, making it inevitable that sooner rather than later it would become the focus of attention for each and every organization involved in anti-drugs enforcement.

Never fight governments, you will always lose. This was the one and only agreed rule between Lisker and Soza.

Lisker's own calculations came through at every turn: his income from the venture was recycled in a large number of legal companies, in a variety of countries, under jurisdictions not linked to each other. The diversification was a vital key to becoming each day closer to Felipe Lisker's ultimate goal – to be the respected and recognised international leader of a family business diversified from its original Colombian coffee business and now involved in a variety of activities, assets and locations. This of course from a flexible holding structure, located in a regularly-changing friendly tax environment.

On this, Lisker took the most direct way to structure his dealings, through Gerstner and his New York law firm. Gerstner understood Lisker's move immediately. They were now even more closely bound together.

In fact Lisker became a properly-referred client of Gerstner's firm at the moment the Mercado Libre Ltd deal was signed and sealed. And when Lenny Gerstner decided to merge his highly-regarded law practice and thus give birth to what was to become Lewman, Applebaum and Fromm, Lisker naturally joined the client roster. This was a key step to Felipe Lisker becoming a legally certifiable and recognized US-managed client.

Some five years before, Felipe had told Soza that he was getting out of the business they were in together. Soza in the meantime had learned a lot from Lisker – he had invested wisely in Brazil, Peru and Argentina, in quoted companies, real estate and anything which helped him to move around freely for investment purposes.

Soza stayed strictly away from the USA. Why try to get involved in a potential hornet's nest of law enforcement? He had no doubt that he ought to be on the law enforcement radar by now, but he rightly gambled that while information gathering was one thing, comparing such information between the DEAs and FBI was still at an early stage. He knew that this was going to end at some time.

By now the origins of the venture had developed into at least five cocaine-producing laboratories, all opening up at different times and hours to ensure they were not spotted or raided. The airstrip at Los Carrizos owned by Mercado Libre Ltd was more active than ever, thanks to US interest in the area. The venture continued through the aftermath of Chile, the Nicaragua situation, the American support for bringing down Pablo Escobar, the Argentinian crises and other not so well-known or documented US government actions in the area. During those years the number of barracks increased until they became a fully-fledged multi-purpose military training facility.

With every political or other crisis, gratitude towards Lisker as a modest coffee grower for his fundamental role in enabling the business to survive was expressed by its representative - Lenny Gerstner.

During their years in business Soza and Lisker would meet for dinner at one of São Paulo's best-known restaurants, A Figueira Rubaiyat on the Rua Haddock Lobo. They would meet whenever a crisis was looming and they received formal information when the airstrip was going to have a serious increase in traffic.

Lisker and Soza's scheme reached its zenith a few years into the venture when Mr Smith requested a conversation with Felipe. At first he thought Smith had found out about the cocaine being shipped out in the Lisker coffee bean bags on their own planes and wanted to be cut into the deal, but he dismissed this thought. If that was the case

Smith would have approached him much sooner and in a different way, and it would have been surely for a cut in the profit for 'assisting' him.

Mr Smith, with his military bearing, came quickly to the point: he had noticed that planes regularly arrived at the strip to be filled with bales of coffee. Perhaps Señor Lisker might have an interest in using the planes arriving at Los Carrizos and flying back empty, usually to the USA and other places where the Lisker coffee might have a market?

For the second time, Lisker couldn't believe his luck. Here was the US government offering him to ship back his coffee beans and cocaine on their aircraft - officially! He could barely keep a straight face when Smith continued to explain that the question had been raised directly by the Mercado Libre owners.

More probably, thought Lisker, a Washington-based budget government official who was aware of the Los Carrizos operation thought it was a waste of public money to let the planes fly back empty after dropping men, equipment, material or whatever at the strip.

He asked where the planes usually landed. Smith answered that they always headed for military-controlled government airstrips or related places, but said the Lisker US organization would be specially permitted on those sites to take deliveries of coffee and any other merchandise.

Lisker asked Smith, through Mercado Libre, to make him a written offer. It came quickly and Lisker accepted it. It was of course handled, executed and coordinated by Lewman, Applebaum and Fromm. Soza couldn't believe it when Lisker told him their merchandise would be arriving in the USA in a totally-controlled environment.

The US government-owned planes flew back to a number of military and private airbases in the area and landed with government identification and instructions, so customs agents were never aware that they were being used on behalf of the government.

In the meantime, since they had started moving drugs in large quantities, Soza had taken care of one specific issue – the security needed for their operations. He had explained that the drugs business was always supported by two pillars, information and security. Information covered everything from knowledge about pricing, quality, distribution, judges, police, anywhere they worked, including knowledge on their end users, who they dealt with and what their competitors were offering. Security covered the entire spectrum of protection, getting paid on time, eliminating anything that could pose a threat, taking care that all merchandise was paid for anywhere they dealt.

There were always people who took the liberty of assuming their suppliers were somewhere in a South American jungle. Special teams were despatched to give quick solutions to such problems. These same clean solutions were always carefully explained to everyone involved, thus making the rules of engagement very clear.

This information unit, consisting of special teams which they named La Unidad, was born the day they put people on watch and started building the Los Carrizos airstrip was build. From then onwards they decided that information retrieval was going to be an even more vital part of their future success. It was to prove the only relevant basis for predicting with a real margin future events or at least making an educated guess.

At first Soza didn't like the vast amount of funds the partners had to put into this information unit, but he accepted it. In addition, on the Brazilian side, Soza had a small army recruited from São Paulo's favelas, mixed with ex military people. These were the people who handled all the practical issues like shipping, protecting the merchandise and issues related to payment collection.

Lisker had proposed to Soza the recruitment of a young Colombian

Army Military Intelligence unit commander by the name of Juan Chepa, who prior to joining the army had lived with his parents at Los Carrizos. The money paid to Chepa by Lisker was in a different league from what he could make in the army, bribes and perks included.

Soza and Lisker detected in Chepa an exceptionally organisational and logistical brain. They asked him to create a compact and highly-disciplined structure to handle everything related to any aspect of security for their operation. Chepa organized La Unidad so that everything was centralised but separated by operating cells. This meant that if a cell or unit was compromised, the problem would stop there.

There were bribes to be arranged, protection to be given, settlements to be made, background checks to be carried out and, last but not least, a low-key but highly capable personal protection team for Felipe Lisker, El Patron. Here too they practised what they preached – Lisker and Soza both had chauffeurs. In reality they both had permanent teams of four, providing constant counter-surveillance. So before Soza or Lisker went to a meeting, the place had been screened, the street swept and all potential danger identified. By handling their security this way they prevented attention being drawn to the arrivals and departures of other drug operators who always seemed to be accompanied by 10 or more security men, openly flaunting their presence and particularly their trade.

Their rapidly increasing success could always give certain people the wrong idea about kidnapping, extortion whatever, but it was all very Colombian.

All this pre-emptive personal security made everybody aware that trying to do something to harm El Patron would be a very dangerous move.

Soza enjoyed a similar set-up in Brazil, also supervised by La Unidad and carefully organized by Chepa wherever they went. La Unidad had grown quickly with their venture and had proved many times to make the difference between life and death, loss or profit.

It was also La Unidad which several years before had taken care of breaking into the Lewman, Applebaum and Fromm offices, after getting from the Peruvian office cleaners all the codes for entering the IT system, specially that of Lenny Gerstner's company and personal files. Through this La Unidad 'exercise', Lisker and Soza obtained black-and-white written confidential information about who was behind Mercado Libre, the billing instructions and the contact parties for this and other parties Lenny Gerstner was acting for.

After La Unidad checked out all these leads, Lisker had all the written proof of the US government involvement he had expected. Not surprisingly, the Los Carrizos operation was one of many handled by Gerstner. It also became clear that Gerstner didn't share this particular client with anybody else.

CHAPTER 13

As recently as three years before, during a dinner at the beginning of March at the Four Seasons in New York, Gerstner had made it crystal clear to Felipe that he was fully aware of the money flows, their origins, his business dealings, its scope and its network of Lisker-supported companies and interests. Lisker of course feigned surprise.

Gerstner was also aware of the flow of transactions going through all the subsidiary companies owned by Lisker in an enormous variety of constituencies, on and offshore, the USA, Europe and of course South America. Their dinner meeting had been as casual as ever; just the regular meeting between a long-standing client account of Lewman, Applebaum and Fromm and the principal partner handling this for the firm.

Felipe had not reacted. He had just listened to Gerstner's detailed overview of his activities. When Lenny finished, they had a frank conversation – a practical business conversation. Gerstner would and could not do anything with the information without getting himself and Lewman, Applebaum and Fromm into a major scandal, jeopardising and eventually ruining everything that had been so carefully constructed over the years.

Why should the rest of Lewmans partners, personnel and clients need to be involved when they had never been part of this Lisker-US Government induced   relationship? And why, Felipe had asked, did Gerstner come forward now?

Age and change at the firm, Lenny answered. Age, he explained, brought a natural urge on his part to clear the past for others to take over. Change, he had continued, because enough was enough. He was a wealthy widower and was to become a retired senior partner of one of Wall Street's most respected law firms. He was already a member of several company boards, patron of various educational trusts and similar. So no, he would not become bored. It was simply time to move on and clear up the past.

The Lisker holding was financially a very healthy company, technically well structured – it would be normal and commendable that when he stepped down at Lewman, Applebaum and Fromm as a partner Felipe Lisker would decide that his holding would need a different council, perhaps with a more American character.

Perhaps it was sad for the firm after all these years, but as he said, it was entirely logical and plausible.

Lisker, after a few moments of thought, had agreed, but he had one request, one condition: would Gerstner mind continuing to be involved in one specific deal - the equity stake building by Lisker in the Spanish bank BANINSA?

Felipe had started buying BANINSA shares through a variety of offshore and onshore investment vehicles about six months before, when Cantarini had organised a meeting in Milan together with Juan de Ronin, the patriarch of the controlling shareholder family and President and CEO of Banco del Norte y Cantabria. Lisker and Cantarini had already met some years before when Lisker had visited Japan on the instigation of Soza, who had fishmeal exports to that market. The fishmeal, and especially the drugs, were handled through the city of Nagasaki by the strong local yakuza clan (bryokudan as described in Japanese literature, violence groups) – the Goto-gumi, a subgroup of the leading Yamaguchi-gumi.

The Osaka based saiko komon –the Goto-gumi senior advisor title - Kazuo Nakanishi had become a trusted local ally to Soza over years of business. It was Nakanishi who, during one of their Japanese visits, presented them both to Cantarini, with whom they clicked immediately.

The setting was typical. Nakanishi had earlier that day introduced them both to his Oyabun – his ultimate boss inside the Goto-gumi – Tadamasa Goto. To celebrate the success of the Goto meeting, Nakanishi had invited Lisker and Soza afterwards for lunch on the top floor of one of Osaka's best hotels. The lunch venue of course was completely sealed by Goto-gumi soldiers. However, as they crossed the hotel lobby towards the special elevators, Kazuo Nakanishi and his security detail suddenly approached an elegantly-dressed man with European features who was sitting reading a newspaper in the hotel lobby. The foreigner immediately rose from his seat, warmly embraced Nakanishi and entered into an animated sotto voce conversation.

Soza and Lisker were waiting some 20 meters away with other members of the Nakanishi security detail and were quietly enjoying the effect the yakuza and his entourage were having when they entered the hotel lobby. It looked as if a total silence had come over the lobby, and the hotel staff were bowed down almost with their faces on the floor.

Nakanishi said something to his so-honbucho, his chief of staff within the Goto-gumi, Yoshi Tanaka, a Harvard-educated lawyer who had handled the logistics with them since they had been in business. He then came over to Soza and Lisker. Tanaka told them that Nakanishi had decided that they would be lunching with the gentleman he presented to them – Giancarlo Cantarini.

After the introductions, the group took the hotel elevators for the ride to the top floor. The hotel staff and other Japanese were still keeping their heads down and avoiding looking in the direction of the Nakanishi party.

Lunch started at 2 pm and ended eight hours later with a Sukiyan table dance. The Sukiyan table dance was a typical way of ending a yakuza lunch. At a certain moment towards the end, a number of beautiful women, one for each man present, disappeared under the large dinner table. One had to avoid showing any reaction to what they did under the table. If you did, you had to pay for the whole meal. Soza paid that day, gladly.

After that first memorable lunch meeting, Cantarini invited Soza and Lisker to Milan. Soza kindly declined, as he wanted only to concentrate on South America, but said his partner would most gladly accept the invitation.

The Milan meeting had also been suggested by Rheinman's Peter Morales. Morales had a long-standing relationship with Giancarlo Cantarini and his family, begun when he had been working at J P Morgan. Cantarini had already become aware of the opportunities Spain was going to present within Europe, and the Spanish duo formed by Diaz and Cortes.

Previous approaches by Italian business tycoons to position themselves had not been a success. The idea that being in the South and having large family holdings would produce easy 'landing strips' for the Italian power brokers proved to be elusive.

Cantarini soon became convinced that Spain and its power élite were different from the Italian social structures of power. Spanish families, unlike those in Italy, were never inclined to work together. For this reason he intensified his relations with Rheinman, who were also actively trying to break into the Spanish market towards the 1992 Barcelona Olympic Games and the Seville World Fair. After that business meeting at the Rheinman Milan offices, later that night at Cantarini's house near the Museo di Storia Naturale, in between the triangle of Corso Venezia with Via Cappuccini and Via Borghetta, Lisker and Cantarini shared a bottle of 1975 Bertani Amarone and worked out a plan to capture the attention and interest of BANINSA's young president Ramon Diaz.

Later on that March night in New York, this was all Lisker remembered as to how his relationship with Diaz had come about.

Gerstner said in the meantime that he would think about a suitable and rational way to execute their relationship within Lewmans, but they would have to agree on who was going to be involved in this transaction. He made it clear that in less than four months he wanted to step back from the firm.

Did Gerstner have somebody in mind, asked Lisker, who could handle his affairs? Gerstner said he had, but he wanted to do it carefully, again so as not to raise any suspicions or sudden scrutiny of their past relationship. It was for their mutual benefit and safety, Lisker had added, but the best cover was that he was going to retire from working at the firm on a day-by-day basis.

So that night at the table at the Four Seasons, they agreed that from the next day Lisker would step-by-step move his business to other law firms. Nothing too drastic or obvious in chargeable hours, but gradually the legal work to be done on BANINSA would act as a perfect attention-grabber for the lawyers at Lewmans.

They agreed that within a year at most, the formal ties between Lewman, Applebaum and Fromm and the Lisker group of companies and its owner Felipe Lisker would be completely severed, coinciding with Gerstner officially retiring.

When they finished their conversation, they looked at each other in silence - a silence which revealed that the unspoken had been stated. Practical business rules had taken care of a typical commercial marriage of convenience between them. The lawyer knew, the client knew. Now age and change needed to be accommodated and their relations brought to an end. Relations whose basic concept and growing results should never see the light of day. A criminal venture which through a combination of Government involvement, clever legal and commercial cover-up and keeping only a very small number of people aware of its existence, had come to fruition. Time had made sure that all traces were made invisible, cleaned out or replaced.

They finished dinner, Lisker insisted on signing the bill, and they walked through the lobby towards the hotel exit on 48th Street. Gerstner's car was waiting at the kerb, its driver already opening its door for him to enter.

They had embraced in that typical crisp New York night of March, looked at each other, and that was it. No words. Gerstner got into his car and closed the door. The driver followed, his door closed and the car drove away.

The next day Lisker began building his relations with other law firms in London and Amsterdam to take the bulk of his dealings away from New York and Lewman, Applebaum and Fromm.

But here and now, Gerstner was dead. And a file had been compiled by him, its exact contents unknown. Files made and kept by people like Gerstner always had one common denominator – if any shit hit the fan, the fallout would create havoc for everybody involved, dead or alive.

Lisker snapped out of his reflections, put his phone away and looked again over the water. Behind him the St Tropez waterfront was filling again as people took their evening stroll and music started to come from the restaurants and bars.

He turned, walked back to Diaz and Cantarini and relit his cigar.

CHAPTER 14

Early summer, 1990

The dark blue Gulfstream IV with the BANINSA logo in gold, blue and red landed at Linate Airport in the early hours of the morning one day at the beginning of July. As soon as the plane came to a stop and its doors had opened, a group of businessmen came down its steps. The last one to disembark was BANINSA's flamboyant President, Ramon Diaz.

A small Mercedes van was waiting, together with a black Audi V8. Near these two vehicles stood a Fiat Croma with three bodyguards standing to attention beside it. A driver opened the door of the Audi and Diaz got in, joining Peter Morales, who had come down with Diaz on the plane that morning after three days of roadshows organized by Rheinman in London, Amsterdam and Edinburgh. These three financial centres presented at that time very much the largest concentration of institutional investors.

The presentations had been very well received. Investment managers, pension fund analysts and portfolio managers alike had a genuine interest in understanding the Virtuvio IPO and the future value of the group and being dazzled by its charismatic president. It was not every day that the analysts and portfolio managers could meet face-to-face with the president of a large Spanish conglomerate who really had a grasp of the businesses his group was in, their margins, their future figures and similar. On top of this Diaz' perfect command of English – always a struggle for Spaniards, then and now – made it a value-enhancing exercise for the investment professionals.

After Milan, they would continue to Paris and finish in Münich before flying back to wherever they were needed. The cars pulled away from the aircraft, heading for the motorway to Milan.

When Diaz sat down, the driver handed him a large manila envelope. He opened it and read through its contents. It was mostly a mixture of short memos concerning Virtuvio's business back in Spain. There was also a drawing by his daughter Sophia which he held up high, laughing and showing it to Morales.

'The notes for the next board meeting!' He joked.

He read on, shifting papers from one hand to the other and stopped.

'Peter' he said after a moment. 'Tonight you will have to excuse me from the dinner meeting with Mediobanca. I need to attend a meeting with Giancarlo Cantarini, who wants to introduce me to Raul Gardini and Mario Schimberni.'

Morales frowned and looked away to hide his reaction from Diaz. Raul Gardini was one of Italy's most influential business people, known by the Salotto Buono as Il Contadino, the peasant. Gardini and his holding company Serafino Ferruzzi controlled 45% of Gruppo Ferruzzi. The other name mentioned, Mario Schimberni, was the controversial president of Montedison, one of Italy's largest industrial groups.

Rheinman and Morales treated such operators very carefully, not so much out of respect but from awareness of the collateral damage they could suffer by doing business with such people, especially in Italy. Italy always had its own rules. Being a member of the EEC was just a practicality, as a large number of investors had found out to their economic disadvantage.

Morales had given up being surprised at the sudden meetings Diaz had with a variety of highly-connected people from all nationalities, with influence reaching into every corner of the global markets, companies and governments. It was typical of Cantarini to put Diaz at the same table as Gardini and Schimberni.

The spectacular house of the Gardini consiglieri Luca di Melo stood between the Corso Venezia and the Via Volfango Mozart, close to the Brea part of Milan. Its neighbourhood was known for the fact that anyone who was anyone in the Milanese business establishment lived there. The house's interior had the unmistakeable style of Versace, mixed with unique works by painters of various generations and styles.

One painting stood out. Placed over a large writing table, it was of Niccolò Machiavelli, sitting at a table in 1520 in Florence. The painter, Santi di Tito, was known to have done several paintings of Machiavelli, but this one was of enormous size and it oozed darkness. People who came to this house knew that there was a clear bond between Luca di Melo, the owner, and the painting.

Di Melo was the one and only personal advisor or consigliero used by Raul Gardini until his death. If you wanted to deal with Gardini, di Melo was the gatekeeper through whom you needed to pass. So it was through di Melo that Cantarini had organised the dinner which had just ended. The six men present, di Melo, Gardini, Schimberni, Diaz, Lisker and Cantarini – walked from the living room through the open doors on to the terrace. The garden was beautifully lit and two big black and white labradors were playing on the lawn. Cantarini and di Melo had been at university together in Padua. Di Melo excelled for his sheer brain power, while Cantarini excelled for his social grace and standing, along with his family holdings.

A real personal friendship had prospered further over the years, joint businesses forming a clear part of the bond. They always met alone and at a number of fixed places if one cared to follow them – either on di Melo's boat near Capri, Cantarini's summer house near Porto Ercole, the Groucho Club in London's Berkeley Square or at the Montcervin hotel in Zermatt, where they had been going skiing during the first week of

February for more than 30 years. Careers after university took off, and though the friends from university roamed the world their relationships continued and developed into an unbreakable trust, especially where the driving forces of business, money and power were concerned. Naturally, both men became godfathers to each others' first-born children.

A butler and a maid were putting out coffee and mineral water bottles on the large oval table, made from a single slab of white marble.

'Can I offer anyone a cigar?' offered di Melo.

Affirmative sounds came from at least four of the men present.

'And would you have some more of that remarkable Amarone which we had?' asked Lisker of the retiring butler.

When everybody had settled, cigars had been lit and glasses had been topped up with red wine a silence settled on the group. It was a warm Milanese July night, but not too hot or humid - a rare treat. Along with the beauty of the garden, produced a mellow atmosphere.

Ramon Diaz carefully put down his glass on the marble table and blew some smoke from his Cohiba cigar. Then he addressed the rest of the table.

'Luca, first of all thanks for once again organising such a perfect dinner' said Diaz.

'Señores, you have all heard that the IPO for Virtuvio is over-subscribed. Our underwriters are being asked to issue more shares. This means our partnership now has a real and established economic value and trading power. After its flotation Virtuvio will be the reference of a new Spanish economic power within Europe and South America. This would not have been possible without your support during these last 12 months.' Diaz left the words floating in the Milan night. 'With your support, we will now consolidate our project so that we can prepare Virtuvio for its next phase – to become a true European conglomerate within five years. This is to you! Sois grande!'

With these words he raised his glass, looked around the table and five glasses briefly touched to join the Diaz toast.

When they settled down again, the conversation quickly turned to the coming holiday season. Di Melo told them of Raul Gardini's new sailing yacht, Il Moro di Venezia, the German Freis design for his assault on the Americas Cup. As di Melo explained, it was not one boat but five, though only one was eventually going to be used by Gardini.

Then Lisker stood up. All heads turned, and the other men raised themselves from their chairs. Cantarini's face lit up as he stepped towards the beautiful woman who had been silently approaching the table from the terrace.

'Ciao Papa!'

'Carla! I thought you were in Sardinia?' said Cantarini.

The butler appeared and put out an extra chair.

Cantarini's daughter made the round of the table, kissing, hugging and laughing with people she had known a long time as close relations of her father over the years she was growing up.

'Tio Luca called me this morning to ask me when I could come by his office to sign the papers which you left me last month, so I thought I would surprise you by coming back earlier to Milan.' She embraced her father and turned to the rest of them.

'When can a young businesswoman like me meet the most powerful men in Southern Europe for free business advice?'

Her laughter was as contagious as her beauty, and both were appreciated by all present. Carla Cantarini was the third of four Cantarini daughters. Their mother had died five years earlier after a long cancer-related disease. All who had known her were in agreement – Carla looked, talked, laughed, argued and moved just like her late mother. Cantarini had met her at university in the USA, and there was clearly pure Sioux bloodstock somewhere in her family origins. This unique beauty had been bestowed on all the Cantarini daughters, but Carla most of all.

Carla was tall at 180 cm and slim and strong, thanks to long and frequent hours of sport. Everybody agreed that she looked like a mixture of Audrey Hepburn and Sophia Loren, and she was gifted with brains and strength from both her parents. At 27, with the international education she had received, Carla was one of the best-kept secrets of European jet-set society. Although she worked closely with her father at his Milan headquarters, she also spent her time travelling the world. She danced at Annabel's in London, skied in Zermatt, attended polo championships in Buenos Aires or lay in the sun on some impressive boat somewhere in the Aegean Sea. Both men and women flocked around her, but the men had an impossible task. She was never seen more than twice with the same man in any publication.

'Bravo! Bravissimo Tio Ramon!' she said as she went from her father's arms towards Ramon Diaz, who she had liked immensely from the first day her father had introduced them during one of their frequent Milan meetings.

'I read it on the plane just now about Virtuvio' she said. 'I want to buy shares right now!'

'Que pena' said Lisker, who was hugging her now. 'Todo vendido. All sold! But I can sell you some at a 15% premium!' Everybody had a good laugh at this and sat down again.

A few hours later, with everybody gone, Cantarini and Diaz were alone with Luca di Melo. The alcohol had now been replaced with still and sparkling water. The sound of Cole Porter drifted from the house.

It was then that di Melo said to both of them: 'When Raul and Schimberni left tonight after dinner, I spoke with them before they got into their car' he said. 'They asked me to convey to you the following for your consideration. Mario is willing to help, but the operation needs to be managed through a stake in Montedison. So they agree to buy 100% of your Iberia de Quimica at the price and conditions as per the Rheinman letter, while you and Cortes will buy a minimum 3% of Montedison. Raul will settle the matter with Gruppo Ferruzzi. Mario will of course arrange the matter with Craxi.'

Diaz slowly inhaled from the cigarette he had just lit. To join forces with Raul Gardini's political family via Gruppo Ferruzzi, plus the blessing of Italy's Craxi government through the backing of Schimberni, meant confirmation of the Virtuvio project. He could hardly contain his joy. This was the turning point for everything he had been hoping for.

Over the last few years, from within the Virtuvio holdings, he and Cortes had worked specifically on making sure that one of the most important holdings and the only chemical company in the portfolio, Iberia de Quimica, was cleaned up, had become well capitalized and had a top-notch management team with a three to five-year business plan to match value expectations. Several of the leading European and American chemical companies came to see them, filed their unsolicited bids and tried to convince them that their price expectations were way out of bounds within the industry, but profits had kept on growing. Now Montedison and the Ferruzzis had accepted their price range for a deal!

'That is very good news, Luca' answered Diaz. 'When will they officially confirm this to Rheinman?'

In putting the question he made it clear to di Melo that all the political implications were first going to be settled between Bettino Craxi, the embattled Italian socialist prime minister and Felipe Gonzalez, Spain's socialist prime minister.

Craxi was trying to expand the Italian chemical state company ENI into the international picture via Montedison. Given the strong influence through the Gruppo Ferruzzi shareholding in Montedison, Gardini was a linchpin. More than anything, Diaz and Cortez knew that with the size of the Virtuvio portfolio companies every move in Spain was anxiously followed by Gonzalez and his Socialist friends. Any sale of the size of an Iberia de Quimica was going through the hands of Gonzalez and his friends. A Montedison operation introduced and handled by a close fellow Socialist soulmate like Craxi was practically impossible for Gonzalez to stop.

This of course including the enormous commissions that were the local standard, needed to implement such an operation in Italy.

'Why don't you come to my office tomorrow with your people and we will agree on a list of steps to be taken' said di Melo. 'If we agree on that I'll handle Peter and Rheinman.'

After Milan and the other visits to the European cities, Rheinman informed the board of Virtuvio that the share issue would certainly be oversubscribed, after four months of heavy sales effort and with the clear deadline that the operation was to end before the European summer. During the same period the Iberia de Quimica acquisition by Montedison was formally declared, accepted by all shareholders and relevant permissions granted by the Italian and Spanish governments. Formal permission was granted by Virtuvio's board to form a strategic core group of co-investors coordinated by Rheinman around Ramon Diaz and Pedro Cortes.

The Virtuvio IPO was one of the highlights of the European financial year. Its proceeds were rapidly assimilated by a Spanish economy thirsty for fresh money and new ideas to increase its capabilities in relation to the European market and its players.

During the years that followed Diaz and Cortes rapidly expanded the Virtuvio portfolio, specially their increased participation and resulting board membership in Spain's leading BANINSA bank. Their partners Lisker and Cantarini were lucky investors – the combination of Virtuvio and Spain's economic ascent in Europe proved to be a happy one.

That is, until the first days of August 1990, when Saddam Hussein invaded Kuwait, thus starting the first Gulf War, and when the world became a different place. The entire world economy was facing a simple yet complex reality: its weakest link – energy in the form of oil - was again going to create utter havoc in every economic scenario. It also meant that the USA was pushed towards its final dilemma: how to control and safeguard oil supplies with countries with whom it had not negotiated seriously for more than 45 years, since the end of the Second World War.

Spain, more than any other European country, felt the impact of the Gulf War immediately. Its dependence on oil imports, the build-up towards the organising of two giant events – the Barcelona Olympic Games and the Seville World Fair – left little to no economic manoeuvring space. As a direct result, Virtuvio needed to stop its acquisitions and put others on hold. Diaz and his management team needed to change tactics quickly. The financial markets in both Spain and Europe were waiting for Virtuvio and Diaz to show a clear path forward in this changed economic landscape.

Felipe Lisker, in the meantime, had decided that 1990 was the year when his agreement with Soza should end. The reason for his conclusion was simple - the international drugs business was getting too much attention.

Men like Pablo Escobar put the drug trade in the public domain through an increasing stream of articles about the violence of the drugs trade. Drugs became associated with people who waged war against governments. With this kind of attention, all kind of details of the money flows related to the drugs trade brought further attention to the various drug lords, logically fuelling further action by governments to crackdown on the trade, wherever and whenever they could.

Lisker had taken care that all his drugs proceeds were onshore in the US and various other European centres, in a myriad structures, companies and investment vehicles. These vehicles owned real estate, cash investments, investment funds, cash and bonds, and were producing a legitimate cash stream. The proceeds of his legitimate coffee business were all invested in Colombia. Lisker took very good care of his coffee workers and their families by building houses and schools for them. His dual life was working well, powered by the healthy streams of cash his drugs investments were throwing off. He had reached a level where he was going to beat the old Colombian saying: drugs dealers never died old or in bed.

Soza again proved to be a practical businessman, and in no time the two partners decided on the separation of their interests, based on the recognition that nobody else could buy Lisker's stake and that participations in the venture concluding didn't work with normal business valuations. Once out of the drugs business or not actively participating, the price of your stake didn't have any bearing on its economics.

The drugs business was like any other. You were in or out, and in this case out usually meant dead. A few exceptions confirmed the rule - Lisker would prove that.

Soza mentioned a price, and Lisker said yes. End of story.

The men agreed that La Unidad would continue to look after any security arrangement or related need by Lisker. The fact that both agreed to this also spelled out the logic of the world they lived in – our joint past is the safeguard for a separated future.

CHAPTER FOURTEEN

They also agreed that if one of them was safe, both were guarded to a certain extent.

CHAPTER 15

New York, 1996

When Paul Anfield left David Fromm he went straight to his office and closed the door. He than called Richard Dunkin, gave his apologies and said he could not make lunch. Then he sat back.

How could you know somebody – think you know somebody - your whole life and yet be so wrong about them? How could Lenny Gerstner have been handling such a situation while maintaining a normal personal and professional life?

Paul looked around his room, a typical lawyer's office. Practically all the available table space was filled with stacks of files. On one side stood a number of photos, one of which was his favourite. It showed Lenny and Paul in front of his grandfather Giuseppe Caruna's house in Sicily and had been taken when the two men had made the trip to the island while attending a meeting in Milan some 15 years or so before. The picture was not going to tell him anything, he thought. He picked up his phone again and dialled his secretary.

'Hi Nancy, listen. Something has come up. Please clean my agenda for the rest of the day. Can you get me Harry Red on the phone?'

'Yes sure Paul, are you OK?' Nancy asked. She had worked for Paul since he had joined the firm and knew him very well.

He assured her he was, and hung up.

Harry Red was Lenny Gerstner's PA. He had worked for Gerstner for his entire professional life, a life which had been devoted entirely to Lewman, Applebaum and Fromm. Harry seemed never to be off duty, 365 days a year. Logic dictates, thought Paul, that if anybody was aware of this situation it would have been Harry.

A light came on his phone. His secretary.

'Paul, I tried him but his voicemail was switched on. I tried his mobile with the same result. Harry hasn't been back to the office since your uncle died, according to Ruth.'

Ruth had been his uncle's secretary for the past few years, since his old secretary had died in a plane crash in the Florida Glades.

'Then do me a favour' he said. 'Please call the Personnel Department and ask them for his home address'.

A little later Paul was in a cab heading for Pike Street on the lower east part of Manhattan. Mid and downtown traffic was the usual crawl, on top of which it had started drizzling and the cab driver was paying more attention to his shortwave radio conversation in a language which was probably known only to a happy few than to his driving. But 20 minutes later Paul was standing in front of a small three-storey brownstone house on Pike Street. He went up the few stairs and rang the doorbell, beside which was a typical security camera intercom. A small copper strip on the door beside the mail slot said 'Red'.

After a few moments, there came a voice behind the front door. 'Yes?'

'Harry – it's me, Paul Anfield.'

Silence.

'Harry? Is that you?'

Still silence.

At last the door opened slightly and Harry looked out. His face revealed that he hadn't had much sleep. His eyes were red and he looked haggard.

'You OK, Harry?'

'Yeah. But please wait and I'll get my coat. I was just leaving.' The door shut again.

A few minutes later, with an overnight bag in his hand, Harry joined

Paul on the pavement. He kept looking nervously around as the two men started walking along the pavement.

'I'm sorry about your uncle' said Harry. 'He was a unique man, Paul.'

As they walked, Harry spoke of the man he had worked with for so long, delivering a eulogy, though his voice sounded nervous.

Harry and Paul had known each for years, but always at a distance. Paul was a junior who quickly became a full partner, while Harry had always remained just an associate.

'Thanks Harry, I appreciate your words' said Paul at length.

Harry was picking up on Paul's pauses. As the two men continued walking along Pike Street towards the River, he became more nervous.

'He was certainly a character, but... why have you come here, Paul? What can I do for you?' Again Anfield didn't reply immediately.

'Does the word Kaneko mean anything to you, Harry?' he said after a pause.

Neither of the men realised as they walked that they were being followed by several pairs of South American eyes. At the moment Paul had arrived at Harry Red's front door, a call had been made from one of the two cars which had been following him. The phone had been stolen a few hours before; it would be destroyed before the day was finished.

'Si?' said the person at the other end.

'El asistente del abogado esta hablando ahora mismo con el primo del abogado. El asistente lleva una bolsa para viajar. Cual son las ordenes?' The lawyer's assistant is talking to the lawyer's cousin. What are we to do?

'Un momento – te llamaré' (I'll call back) and the line went dead.

After roughly a minute the stolen cellphone rang.

'El asistente no ha entregado nada al primo?' The assistant didn't give anything to him?

'No - de momento hablan, el bolso no fue abierto.' They are only talking, the bag hasn't been opened.

'Termine el asistente. Solo el asistente. Confirma?'

'Vale – solo el asistente.'

The line went dead. The man on the phone left the Lincoln he was driving, crossed Pike Street and tapped on the window of a Ford Galaxy. Both cars had been stolen a week ago from a long-stay car park somewhere in Midtown and their licence plates changed.

'Solo el asistente, el otro sin tocar' he said. Only the assistant, don't touch the other.

As he turned back towards the Lincoln, three doors of the Ford Galaxy opened and a man emerged from each. The trio moved in unison, like trained soldiers ready to enact an endlessly-practised drill. Anfield and Harry Red were a hundred meters in front.

The three men began to talk animatedly in Spanish as they closed the distance to Paul and Harry. The other man had stepped back into the Lincoln, which was crawling along the kerb slightly in front of the four men. From the window of the Lincoln, you could hear a scanner tuned into NYPD.

Anfield and Harry Red kept on walking, unaware of the approaching men.

'Kaneko? No, I don't think so.'

'Harry – what was Lenny working on these last few months ?'

'Er... let me think. Yep, the Monsanto case. Also he had been asked to act for the Culver committee, his usual dealings with Bear Stearns and....'

'Felipe Lisker?' interrupted Paul.

Harry's reaction was more audible than visible.

'Lisker - now why does that ring a bell?' he answered.

'Kaneko was the filename Lenny used to detail all the dealings concerning a man named Felipe Lisker, a company named Mercado Libre and the relationship between Lisker, the company and the US Government' said Paul. He waited for a response. Harry Red lowered his head with a sigh.

'Paul, I swear to you I didn't know what this was all about' he said. 'Yes, I knew he had frequent contact with Lisker but I never knew what it was all about. Your uncle only told me that it was an old personal relationship from before the time Lewman existed. It was just a favour. When I found out one day that we billed them like a full client, I became confused.'

He stopped and turned to Paul.

'I asked him one day and said 'Lenny - what's this about? What do we do for Lisker?' but he said that I should forget it. The very next day, all the files on Lisker were suddenly lifted from central document keeping. I never saw them again. This was about three years ago. During that time, Lisker came only two or three times a year to see your uncle, and never at the office. And no, I didn't ask further. It simply wasn't my business.'

Now two of the three men following had passed them, without drawing the attention of either Paul or Harry, who were still immersed in their conversation. The third man was now directly behind Anfield.

'So nobody ever had a look at this Kaneko file except my uncle? No secretary, nobody?' continued Paul.

'Nobody. After meetings with Lisker, Lenny just put in documents or meeting notes or whatever was relevant, but then he would take them out again, usually the next day. He gave standard invoicing instructions to the administration; the bills were always paid in record time, so no-one ever bothered.'

'How do you mean – he would take them out again?' asked Anfield.

'He scanned them and attached them to the file. He kept the originals, but not in the office files. I know, because of the increase in bytes on the file. When IT maintenance came by a few months before he passed away all the data files were checked and cleaned, so I had a look at various files which were going to be deleted from the partners' data files to central backup.'

Paul was familiar with this procedure. In a large law firm like Lewmans it was standard IT procedure, to ensure PCs didn't become overloaded with non-essential data for past cases, closed cases or any data which took up large quantities of memory space.

'So the file is still on his PC?'

'Technically, yes, but something strange happened a few days ago' answered Red. 'Two guys from the IT department came by and took your uncle's workstation away. They came back a few hours later and asked first Ruth and then me where Lenny's PC was. The strange thing was that they knew the exact brand and model of your uncle's machine. '

'So?'

'In a company with more than 900 employees? I thought it was strange. Ruth in the meantime called IT and they told her nobody from there had been ordered to retrieve anything from Lenny's stuff. So when these guys came back with the workstation and asked for the PC, I decided to keep it. I told them it was probably in Lenny's apartment. They took a long look at me and Ruth but they left when Ruth asked them who had sent them.

'I didn't think anything more of it, but the day after Lenny's funeral the same two guys came by my house. I watched them through the security camera on my front door. I recognised one of them - he had a scar over his left eyebrow. I asked myself - why were they coming to my house? Of course I didn't open the door.'

'That's why you're nervous?'

'Is that obvious?'

Before he could reply, Paul was interrupted by a savage blow to his left ear. He fell to the pavement, stunned. As he hit the pavement the two men who had passed them turned round and simultaneously drew automatic weapons with silencers. They fired together.

Harry had no time to speak. He fell back as two 9mm bullets from a silenced Heckler & Koch P10 struck his head. One of the bullets carried away bone and brain tissue in a fine spray of blood.

The two men stepped towards the fallen men. One of them took the overnight bag from Harry's hand, and all three stepped toward the waiting Lincoln. The car pulled quietly away, followed some seconds later by the Galaxy, which had been waiting on the other side of the street.

It was all over in 30 seconds. Pike Street at that time of the day was practically empty, and it was some time before a man walking his dog came upon the scene.

Some four blocks to the east, the two cars involved were distancing themselves from the scene. Inside the Lincoln, one of the men opened Harry's bag. He lifted out the file of papers and handed them to the man sitting in front, who started leafing through them. Then he put them back, picked up his phone and pressed redial.

'Si?'

'Son los papeles. Es un tipo de diario y contiene todo, escrito a mano. Fechas, operaciones, nombres, cuentas y cosas similares'. Dates, operations, numbers.

'Okay – nos veremos en la casa.'

'Mid town o lo del Downtown?' the man in the Lincoln asked.

'Mid town.' The call ended.

Back at the scene, Paul's rescuer helped him to a sitting position. He found himself looking into the eager eyes of a yellow labrador. He was being told not to move, but he wasn't about to. His head felt as if it had been hit by a train.

Paul looked the other way and saw Harry Red on his back with eyes open and a pool of blood oozing from his head.

Sitting up only made him feel worse.

'Don't move – the medics will be here shortly' said the dog's owner.

Paul heard police sirens. Shootings in New York in broad daylight could be relied on to generate a quick response.

CHAPTER 16

A few hours later, having been checked over by the ambulance people and given statements to a variety of police officers, Paul was back in his office. He had told them all he was fine.

Paul knew one thing as he headed back - the target had been Harry, and Harry only. The bag had gone. No witnesses had seen the attack. It must have been a professional job; highly-disciplined professionals with clear orders.

He asked Nancy for a clean shirt, went to the washroom to wash his face and hands and returned to his office. He said nothing about the shooting to her or to anyone else at the office, but he knew full well that by tomorrow morning at the latest everybody would know about the killing.

Now Paul had only 15 minutes before he had to go up to see David Fromm and attend the partners' meeting that would be following.

What was going on? His uncle had died. Then 48 hours later, a file he had prepared, documenting years of a trade-off for US military covert operations against drugs had appeared on the table. Then his uncle's PA for more than 25 years stopped coming to work, and when he had left his house he had been gunned down in broad daylight. Yet they had let Paul get away with a bump on the head.

Uncle Lenny must have been having dealings for years, dealings which he had shared with nobody. None of it made sense.

David Fromm would have liked to use the 'ammunition' of the killing of Harry Red to cut Paul loose, in the interests of the partnership. Not going to see him and not showing up at the partners' meeting would not change anything. His own position had become a problem.

120

He made a decision. He needed to find out what the real story was behind his uncle's dealings, and he had to do it alone.

He picked up his laptop and a few papers and left the office, telling Nancy that he would be in touch. Something about the way he spoke told her not to ask any questions. She nodded, and watched him heading for Fromm's office.

In a brownstone somewhere between East 50th Street and the river, the man from the Lincoln handed over Harry Red's bag to Juan Chepa, the man in charge at La Unidad. Then he sat down and waited. He knew that the Lincoln, which they had abandoned somewhere in Harlem, would be stripped bare of all evidence by thieves within 24 hours.

Chepa went through the diary and papers from the bag. Harry Red had been – not surprisingly – a meticulous administrator. Everything related to the Kaneko business was reflected in the diary.

After 15 minutes he put the papers down. How many copies were there? If the Harry Red fellow had kept a written score, how many others had them? Gerstner was sure to have had one. But was that the only one? And where and how had the handwritten files been transferred? Impersonating IT staff and removing the computer had produced nothing.

The only two confirmed sources of the material were gone – Gerstner had gone through natural causes and they had taken care of Harry Red themselves. Did the young lawyer, the one who was related to Gerstner, know anything? Why had he called at Red's house?

The chair Chepa was sitting in was a reflection of the rest of the house. Modern, spartan and with no specific character. Strictly functional. Just like the brownstone itself - a functional safe house for La Unidad. Bought a number of years ago through one of Soza's dummy companies and refurbished with rather tasteless furniture.

Naturally the house was protected by a state-of-the-art alarm system, installed by a firm whose owners were ex-Colombian special forces and who had stayed in the US after working for the CIA as support in the War on Drugs. Working for La Unidad on specific occasions was however very lucrative.

Soza and certain others who were permitted to do so stayed at the brownstone on certain occasions, always with a low profile. Neighbours and others just needed to know that the house belonged to a rich South American who sometimes came to New York on business, and that his staff now and then came to look after the property. It brought discretion and easy explanations.

Chepa had left the man from the Lincoln sitting in the living room and had walked via the hallway to the end of the house, passed through the large kitchen and opened the door to a garden. He sat down on a small bench, took a mobile phone from his pocket and dialled a number from memory.

'Si?'

'What do you want us to do?'

'Cual es tu opinion?'

'He knew everything that would make him a liability. Dates, transfer amounts, who signed what, everything. I don't know who else had access to the information. The lawyer and his assistant have been accounted for.'

'The young one?' the voice came back.

'From the wires we are sure he was never involved by his uncle in any of the dealings' said Chepa.

Silence. Then:

'Keep him under wraps 24/7. Drop the documents in Miami on your way back.'

'Si, Patron.'

The line went dead. Chepa went back into the house and gave new instructions to the man from the Lincoln.

David Fromm had been informed five minutes before by the NYPD of the shooting of Harry Red and Paul's presence at the crime scene. The conversation between Paul and David was brief. Paul explained to David why he had gone to see Harry. They discussed what they should do next.

'Paul, given the full involvement of your uncle in the matter at hand, I would like you to investigate this situation and the firm's possible situation past and present and explore what strategy we should follow. I'll propose this at the partners' meeting. I'll ask for help for you on the cases you're handling at the moment, if you wish. You're OK on this?'

The partners' meeting took more than two hours. Most of the time was spent discussing business transactions in hand. Only at the end did Fromm explain in a few brief lines what had happened since he had received the Kaneko file that morning, and tell them about the killing of Harry Red.

Paul watched the other partners' faces as Kaneko was mentioned, but he could detect no reaction. The news of Harry's murder produced the expected reaction, especially with the more senior partners who had known him as PA to his uncle almost since the firm had been founded.

When the meeting had finished he left the office, crossed 52nd Street and took a right into Park Avenue. It was not raining, but the rush hour had come and he felt like walking. He wanted to gather his thoughts and plan - plan what to do next to work out what the Kaneko file meant, understand the life of his uncle and why he had done what he had done. How had Lenny got involved in this?

He had walked several blocks along Park Avenue when he suddenly saw her. She was dressed differently but it was definitely the woman in red he had seen at the funeral. She was getting out of a black Mercedes in front of the Four Seasons hotel. The same Jeep Cherokee was close behind, the same security people standing by.

The woman crossed the pavement and went into the hotel lobby. The security people got back into their cars and drove off.

On an impulse, Paul decided to follow her. He went into the hotel. The woman was going up the stairs to reception, where she spoke briefly to somebody behind the desk and received a package. Then she turned back and walked towards the hotel bar.

As usual at this time of the day, the bar was crowded with after-work drinkers, visitors to New York finishing their day, business people having a last conversation before heading home or to the gym.

The woman was immediately escorted by a waiter towards a corner table. Paul waited until she was seated and then he walked over. Close up she looked even more beautiful. She was tall and her jet-black hair fell over her shoulders. She was dressed in tight faded light blue jeans, a black turtle-neck sweater – cashmere most probably – and a black leather man's jacket. She wore little make-up and had on large golden earrings and a Daytona Rolex, again a man's style. On her feet were old-fashioned, well-worn cowboy boots.

'Excuse me.'

'Yes?'

Her light green eyes held Paul's gaze. She looked on her guard, but she also recognised that the man who had approached her didn't seem to present any immediate danger.

'We met yesterday.'

'Yesterday?'

'At the funeral of Lenny Gerstner.'

'Ah! Yes of course. And you are?'

Her accent sounded slightly South American, not European Spanish.

'Paul Anfield. Lenny was my uncle.'

A waiter approached and asked them what they wanted to drink. She ordered a glass of white wine, and Paul followed suit. When the waiter had left, they looked at each other.

'At least it is one of the better opening lines – 'didn't we meet at a funeral'?'

They both laughed. 'Do you mind? said Paul, indicating the chair opposite her.

'Of course! No problem.' When she smiled she displayed a perfect set of white teeth.

'Carolina Monterey.' She held out her hand; it was firm and strong.

'So what was your connection with my uncle, if I may ask?'

'Your uncle had been a dear friend of my family for a very long time. He handled our family's corporate legal affairs for more than 30 years. It was only right that I should represent them and pay our respects to him. My father couldn't come, unfortunately.'

She explained further. Lenny had managed legal affairs for her family in the US. Her family had come from Colombia but had based part of its business in New York and Miami at the beginning of the Sixties. She worked and lived between Miami, Cali and Madrid, from where she administrated her family's European activities as a type of family office.

'And what does Mr Paul Anfield do, apart from approaching girls in bars just because he has noticed them at funerals?' she asked with a twinkle in her eye. Paul laughed and explained his position at Lewman, Appelbaum & Fromm. They talked; they ordered more wine.

Paul was impressed by Carolina Monterey. It very soon became clear that she knew all about business, finance and art. She had travelled the world and clearly knew exactly what she wanted. She also happened to be very beautiful.

He felt like a small boy who didn't want the moment to go away. He plucked up his courage.

'Are you free for dinner tonight, by any chance?'

She waited a moment, looking him in the eye. Her expression was serious, but a smile was playing with the corners of her mouth.

'Well, well Mr. Anfield. That's very fast!'

She seemed to consider for a moment.

'I'd love to, but I promised to go out with my family tonight. Tomorrow I'm flying back to Miami.'

'Perhaps next time, when you're back' said Paul. He signalled the waiter for the bill.

They talked some more. It seemed they both liked the same sports - golf, tennis and sailing. They agreed that the South of France was the best place in the world in summer with a boat. Ibiza came second, Sardinia third.

The bill came, Paul paid cash and got up.

'Thank you Paul. That was nice'

'The pleasure was mine.'

Each waited for the other, not sure what to do next. In the end they settled for a handshake. This made them laugh, so Paul kissed her hand.

He turned and walked away. But as he was going down the stairs towards the hotel exit he heard her voice calling his name, and the familiar clack-clack of cowboy boots on the hotel's marble floor. It was Carolina.

'Tonight after dinner we're going with my family and a group of people to Mumba Mumba in the village – why don't you join us?'

Paul had been to Mumba Mumba several times. It was the hottest place in New York right now, three floors of dancing, dining and lounging with a very strict door policy. If you didn't have an invitation it would take a miracle to get you in. Fortunately Paul did have a miracle. One of the owners of Mumba Mumba had a brother working as a junior associate at Lewmans offices.

'And will you tell your family what a feeble excuse I used to hook up with you?'

She laughed. Paul said he would see her at Mumba Mumba some time after midnight. He left the Four Seasons, called for a cab and asked the driver to take him to his gym near the Park.

From the cab, he made a few phone calls and checked his messages. He had decided that Carolina Monterey was a woman he wanted to know better.

CHAPTER 17

When Paul reached THM – The Human Machine, one of New York's top gym & spa venues – he had completely forgotten about one thing. He hadn't called Deborah White. Deborah and Paul had been seeing each other for about three months, after having met at a dinner at the home of mutual friends.

The attraction had been mutual and primarily physical, with no strings attached. Deborah was from an old Bostonian family, and she worked as PA to some kind of fund management wizard near Wall Street. She had a clear view that New York was just a stopover, not a last port of call for a 24-year-old woman with brains and an interest in seeing the world outside the USA and especially outside Boston. She had no interest in forming a lasting relationship of any kind. She was young, intelligent and great fun to be with.

Deborah looked like a double of Cindy Crawford, without the pimple. In men she looked for the four Gs – good looking, good laughs, good intelligence and good sex. With her own looks, she never had to settle for anything less.

Paul Anfield had proved to Deborah over these last months that he was a 4G. They both led hectic lives, so there was no specific routine – no fixed times or places. When there was time, they saw each other. It was as simple as that.

THM was crowded when Paul entered the men's locker room. They had told him in reception that they were at full capacity, and that Deborah was already playing a game of squash with one of the teachers. She was an exceptional racket player. Whether it was tennis, squash or racket ball, she had a natural feeling for the ball and what could be done with it within the lines and the rules.

Paul went to his locker, said hello to those around him he knew, and changed into sports gear. The painkillers he had given by the ambulance people that afternoon were still having an effect.

He did some stretching and warm-up exercises, and decided to take a look at the squash courts. THM had an enormous gym hall with each and every exercise machine available, an Olympic size pool and a full beauty spa, plus five squash and three racket ball courts. Behind the squash courts, you could sit and watch the games.

In one of the squash courts, Deborah was making life very difficult for one of the club trainers. Her strokes had speed, strength and a great deal of intelligence. She waved at Paul between points.

After a few minutes the club professional managed to finish off the game by moving Deborah to the left front side of the court during their final rally. She tried a drop shot, but the pro had anticipated this. He played a perfect lob to the right-hand back corner of the court, where the ball died.

When they came off the court, the club pro greeted Paul and headed to the locker rooms. Deborah said down on the bench beside Paul. She took a few moments to catch her breath, Paul drying her perspiring face with a towel.

'So why did you lose?' asked Paul with a good-humoured smile while kissing her brow.

Deborah answered by lightly wiping her sweating forehead on his.

'I didn't want to win again, it would reflect badly on the level of squash professionals at THM' she answered between gulps of air. She got to her feet and started her after-match stretching. 'You didn't call. Or did I miss you?'

Paul wasn't sure whether to tell her about the day's events. Not that he didn't trust Deborah, it was simply that their relationship hadn't really got further than two young people enjoying the New York life together. They talked plenty, but their personal lives had not yet really become one of their topics.

'Just one of those days at the office – sorry.'

'Do we have anything on tonight?' Deborah finished her stretching session. 'I was thinking of having dinner later with some friends and then turning in early. I've got to fly to Boston tomorrow, got some meetings.'

He got up, kissed her and put the towel over her head.

'Don't worry. I'm going to have a game myself if there's somebody to play with. If not I'll do some running and go home'.

She put her arms around him, pulling him close and kissing him. Then she looked into his eyes and frowned.

'You're OK?' she asked. She had had enough physical contact with him to be able to tell when things were not quite right.

Paul kept her close and held her gaze, enjoying the scent he liked so much - the combination of lingering perfume, soap and sweat. Clean sweat produced by a body which was used to sport, unlike the sweat of those who don't make enough physical effort to sweat regularly.

'Why shouldn't I be?' he answered, moving his head to the nape of her neck and sliding his hands down to her buns . He massaged them softly.

'Hmm. Yep! A little lower! Nothing like your hands, Mr Lawyer.'

She began to grind her body against his, and his penis immediately started to come to life, proving that sex always overcomes any other preoccupation in a healthy man's mind and body.

'Miss White' Paul murmured in her ear, slowly sucking on her earlobe. He had found out the first time they had kissed how much that aroused her.

'Yes Mr Anfield?'

'Your mother and father are pillars of the Boston society. Do they know their daughter is engaging in soliciting lewd acts, performed in a public space?' He looked around to make sure nobody was getting a free look at their increasingly heavy petting. Seeing that nobody was watching, he slipped his hands inside her shorts.

'Aah - foul!' gasped Deborah. One of his fingers lightly caressed her through her panties. He lightly massaged the outer lips of her vulva.

She slid her hand inside Paul's trousers and took hold of his shaft. It had now come fully to life. This was one of the key elements of the relationship between them: grab the moment. Everything else could wait.

Paul gasped softly into her ear as she started to move her hand up and down his shaft.

'Miss White, we are in a public place' Paul whispered in her ear, smiling at the fire they had lit so quickly.

'Make up your mind, Mr Lawyer – me, now, or an uncertain game of squash?' She reached for his scrotum. His defences were almost gone.

'Foul play – is that what you want, Miss White?' Paul had moved her panties to one side and had entered her, his finger moving towards her clitoris.

Deborah suddenly pushed him back, withdrawing her hand from his shaft and his pants. He let go of her at the same moment.

She took his hand, now wet with her sweat and juices, and pulled him along, picking up her gear.

'Come on – I've got a key.'

Paul didn't ask questions. He followed her, knowing that when Deborah had an urge it was better not to argue. They went through a temporary side door, the entrance to the new, as yet unopened part of the THM spa section. Its construction was reaching the last stage; it would be open to THM members in less than a month.

She closed the door behind them and kept going, clearly knowing her way. They made a left turn, passed through more doors.

Then Deborah stopped, took a key from her purse and opened a door into a room which was filled with towels, bathrobes and other assorted pre-packed linen, ready for the opening. In the middle was a large table, clearly being used for folding purposes.

'How did you know...?' began Paul, but he was cut off. Deborah turned and in one movement she had thrown her personal stuff aside and drawn Paul into a kiss, preventing him from saying anything more. She removed her sweat-soaked shirt in one pull, followed by her sports shorts and panties. Then she jumped on to the table, moved her hands behind her back and opened her white sports bra, leaving her firm breasts exposed and waiting.

'Action time, Mr. Lawyer!'

20 minutes later she was lying on top of Paul, still on the table, stroking his face. The room smelled of a mixture of fresh paint, newly-starched linen, sweat and love juice.

They looked at each other.

'Well – we've inaugurated the new extension before the club's president had the chance to do it' Paul said softly. She giggled and held him close, not noticing that Paul's mind was already somewhere else.

As he left THM an hour later (he had somehow managed to find the energy for a game of squash as well), Paul failed to notice a dark blue Lexus parked near the building with two people in the front. It drew away and followed the cab Paul was taking, downtown towards the Village.

Paul got to Mumba Mumba to find a long queue at the entrance. He walked up to one of the doormen, embraced him, asked him how he and his family were doing, and was led straight into the club. The man was the brother of one of the post boys at the Lewmans office and specifically somebody who Paul had helped. Paul never had a problem getting into Mumba Mumba.

The Lexus found a spot opposite the club's entrance. It waited there, engine idling.

Inside, Paul walked through the restaurant part and entered the club lounge, next to the enormous dance hall. The place was full. Salsa music was booming off the walls and the air filled with laughter as New York's finest chatted and bustled around.

Paul went to the girl in charge of the lounge part of the club and asked if she had a reservation under the name of Monterey. She did not.

He scanned the lounge thoroughly, but there was no sign of Carolina. He thanked the girl and made his way to the large bar in the dance hall part of the club. He had to wriggle between people standing and talking and avoid waiters with their trays, but finally he found a spot at the bar, caught the attention of one of the barmen and ordered a spritzer, with more white wine than soda water. Drink in his hand, he watched the crowds.

Fully relaxed by sex and squash, Paul wasn't concerned that he couldn't immediately find Carolina Monterey. He was just enjoying the view, the sights and sounds of a typical slice of New York night life. Mumba Mumba felt alive, just because of the people who moved around the place. You had to be young, you had to be cool, and who cared about tomorrow?

Then he felt a hand on his arm. Carolina stood behind him, partly obscured by another person. Paul turned. She stepped away from the people she was apparently with and moved closer.

'So how was dinner with the family?'

'Like a family dinner should be – fun! So what did you do?'

'I managed to sweat the New York daily routines away' Paul answered.

She hadn't changed her clothing. She still looked as impressive as she had earlier. Again he felt as he had felt when he left the Four Seasons earlier: don't stay too long near this woman. She is too beautiful for a man like you.

'Let me introduce some of my family' said Carolina. She turned back to the group standing behind her, tugging him along. He smiled as she did the introductions. They seemed a pleasant bunch - some were her brothers and sisters, some married, some single, with or without girlfriends. They all greeted him in the open way only Latin people seem to have.

He began chatting to one of her older brothers, who explained that he worked for a leading Mexican brokerage house on Wall Street. The talk quickly turned to business gossip. Carolina began talking to one of her sisters, but she caught Paul's eye once or twice as if to make sure he was enjoying himself.

The Monterey family seemed to be a close-knit one. Though they moved around from continent to continent for personal, professional or other reasons, they always made sure that at least once a month a gathering was organised at one of the family homes. A number of the brothers and sisters seemed to work for the family holdings, while others had made independent careers.

After a few rounds of drinks, the group decided to go midtown to check out a new salsa club they had been told about.

'Were they were nice to you, Mr. Paul Anfield?' a smiling Carolina asked Paul, taking his arm as they headed for the exit.

'I didn't know you liked gardening' he said. 'If you'd told me that I would have told you about my mother's place in New Jersey.'

'Gardening? Who told you that?' she said, surprised.

'Give me your hands' he said. He caught her hands, brought them up to his face and studied them. 'Yup! See? Typical green fingers! Garden hands, hands that have worked the earth!'

Only then did she see that he was smiling.

They stood by the long line of hopefuls trying to get in and limos and yellow cabs milling about for passengers.

'Thanks for tonight, Carolina' he said, placing an elegant kiss on her hand.

'CAROLINA! Ven! Vamos!' came a shout from one of her brothers, whose car had been fetched by the parking valet. Carolina took his hand and tried to pull him along.

'I'd better drop out now' he said. 'Tomorrow is a busy day.'

'Either that's one of your better lines or you're really serious, Mr Lawyer' she replied.

'I'm serious' he said. 'And I would like to chase you, Miss Monterey.'

They both laughed.

'I'll call you. What was the name of your firm again?' she said with a smile, though she already knew the answer.

'Lewman, Applebaum – they're in the book, useful guys to know. Not cheap.' He answered back with a straight face.

Cars were honking and souped-up V8 engines growling. Full-blast salsa music was coming from their open windows. The usual paparazzi were looking on as always at this hour of the New York night, hoping to catch a well-known face who might be leaving the club worse for wear.

Paul walked Carolina to one of the cars, where one of her brothers had opened a rear door. The music of Ruben Blades was coming out, at levels which could easily damage the eardrums.

'El guapo no viene?' her brother quizzed her from the window. The handsome man is not coming?

'El guapo, hermano mio, es un tipo serio con responsabilidades por la mañana.' He has things to do tomorrow.

'Que huevon!' the brother laughed. Stupid man.

'Hasta pronto, señor abogado' she said, giving him a peck on the cheek. She got into the car and the driver saluted Paul and roared away, followed by several other cars.

Paul found a yellow cab, gave the driver directions home and started to think about Carolina Monterey.

Behind the cab, unseen by Paul, the dark blue Lexus followed.

CHAPTER 18

The next morning Paul was at the office at 0800 sharp, dressed in a Paul Stuart dark blue suit cut from Italian cloth, with a plain white handkerchief in his breast pocket. His white shirt had been made to measure in London. He wore no tie. On his feet was one of his usual pairs of black Gucci loafers.

Although he was not naturally a snappy dresser – contrary to the impression he always gave to people – he had been taught by his father and uncle that it came with the territory; of business, of being a lawyer, and of working with people who judged you at first sight by the way you were dressed.

His Uncle Lenny had taken him to Milan and London when he had joined the firm and explained to him in Harvey & Hudson's that there were London shirt makers and there were shirt makers who were ex London. The difference was in the style of cutting. Paul had remained a Harvey & Hudson client ever since. Italian hand-made shirts were just that – Italian. The typing pool and the other staff at Lewmans had voted him the firm's snappiest dresser on the day he had started working there, and he had kept the title unofficially ever since.

First he dealt with all the emails and voice messages that had come in since he had left his desk the previous day. On his desk there were also a number of internal memos, plus a message from the Metropolitan police with a request to call a certain detective regarding the killing of Harry Red.

Another note said that the Kaneko files were waiting to be picked up from David Fromm's personal secretary's desk, specifying that they would be given only to him personally.

He got up, went over to see the girl in question at Fromm's offices and returned to his own. On his way back he first took care that the case files he was busy on were handed to his fellow partners. During the morning he would call them to give background where needed.

He gave instructions not to be disturbed, switched off his cellphone and started reading the Kaneko file from start to finish.

After more than two hours of solid reading, making notes, checking those notes against internet searches and papers from the firm's own library, he got up, grabbed his phone, switched it on and left his office. His head was swimming with information. The best way to put it all in order was to get some fresh air. He took the elevator down, went out of the building and started walking.

A number of issues regarding Kaneko had become very clear. The first was that for a very long time Lewmans had been working directly, through his Uncle Lenny, for a massive criminal scheme which was led by a certain Felipe Lisker. Drugs were his main business, though his name did not seem to appear in connection with drugs anywhere on the web; only with the coffee trade.

Drugs created enormous amounts of cash, which was then recycled through a structure of onshore and off-shore companies all over the world. Nothing new there, except perhaps for one very specific feature – the indisputable participation from the very start by the US Government, through people acting for it.

Why his uncle had participated in this one hundred per cent illegal venture was a mystery. Lenny had been the type of man for whom right and wrong were usually simple matters. When clients of Lewmans had chosen wrong over right and thus needed defence, it was never a subject of discussion. People came to the firm to right a wrong.

How can you defend people when you know they have committed a crime? That had been one of the topics he had discussed with his uncle when he had first joined the firm.

His cellphone went off. Unknown number from the New York area.

'Yes?'

'Mr. Paul Anfield?'

'Speaking.'

'Detective Wainfield of NYPD Homicide. I left a message at your offices yesterday.' The typical Brooklyn drawl came over the cellphone. He had forgotten to call them back.

Wainfield asked him if he could call at No 1 Police Plaza later that afternoon. Paul answered that he would be there, and after checking which floor Wainfield was located on he finished the call and walked back to his office. On the way he asked for some sushi takeaway to be ordered from the Japanese restaurant below the office.

Once in his office, he took out a yellow pad and started to work, the Kaneko file beside him. An hour of concentrated work later, he leaned back in his chair and held up the pages he had written and the lines connecting people, facts and relationships.

The Kaneko file was nothing less than a detailed review by Lenny Gerstner of the trails left behind by a number of parties involved big time in whitewashing funds which had come from the drugs trade, or were directly related to it. The other manila envelopes were stuffed with copies of banking transactions, transfers, company deeds, instructions received, photographs and handwritten notes by his uncle.

It took him a few more hours to come up with the basics. The trail started in Washington at the end of the 1970s, when Lenny Gerstner had been approached by Senator Peter Brooks, then head of the permanent Inter-America Security Committee. Brooks had always met his uncle with a certain John Cushing, then an assistant director for the CIA. Lenny Gerstner, for reasons not clear to Paul, had after a few conversations started to act on their behalf.

Just like that. No notes, no indication of what had moved Gerstner to initiate his activities for Brooks and Cushing. Only that, according to the copy bank statements, a certain company called Kaneko Ltd, registered on the Isle of Man in the UK, had become a fee-paying client to the firm which was handled exclusively by his uncle. Paul had put a big question mark against this.

Companies were set up, funds were transferred within and outside the US. Then the next step was his uncle surfacing in Colombia.

Copies of faxes and telexes – still used in South America even then – mentioned the sale and leaseback of a large tract of land by Lisker's family to a Bahamian - domiciled company called Mercado Libre Ltd. A copy of the transaction document mentioned the type of work that was going to be undertaken, specifically the construction of an airstrip and various buildings.

In the file were copies of where the money originated from and how, via Gerstner, it had been wired to Lisker. There were wire transfers to a myriad accounts through 20 banks or more all over the world.

One document in the file was a copy of a letter by Cushing dated about eight months after the Colombian land transaction, asking on behalf of the Inter-America Security Committee if Gerstner and his firm would help Lisker to establish a number of companies on US soil. Although the letter was stamped 'Private & Confidential' and came from a senate-appointed committee, its contents contained more about instructions than soliciting professional help for and on behalf of a 'friend' of the Government of the USA.

The actual transactions were conducted initially from Colombia and led by Felipe Lisker. In the years following, all kinds of companies appeared and disappeared acting on his behalf. Lisker had been in written contact with his uncle, clearly based on the sheer arrogance of knowing that this all was covered by the US Government. To further illustrate this, there were almost yearly notes signed by Cushing and/or Brooks to express their gratitude for Lenny's help and support in helping Lisker. The notes were always written on US Government paper, such as special committee letterheadings.

The cover for the drugs production and cultivation had been - coffee farming. Paul soon found through the web that the locations of the Lisker estates were of vital interest to the US State Department, who needed a base for covert operations to support the struggle against communist-inspired guerilla movements in the area.

At four o'clock he left the offices and took a cab to No 1 Police Plaza for his meeting with Wainfield. Again the dark blue Lexus followed him downtown with the three men inside. If he had been more alert, Paul would have noticed that he had been followed ever since leaving his apartment that morning. Paul Anfield didn't have that type of attentiveness, and the people shadowing him knew that. Even so they never forgot their training or became over-confident.

When Paul reached No 1 Police Plaza he signed in, passed security control and was escorted to the fifth floor, where he was shown into a small conference room. After a few minutes Detective Raymond Wainfield appeared. He introduced himself and slapped a file on the table.

Ray Wainfield looked the part of a tired New York law enforcement officer. His questions were to the point, and mainly concentrated on two matters – how well did he know Harry Red, and was there anything he could remember before Harry got shot. Just professionally, answered Paul, and no, nothing had struck him as odd. Wainfield continued with several more questions, and after 20 minutes the conversation seem to be coming to an end. Paul was wondering why he had been asked to come - he had already given all this information in a statement.

Finally the interview was over and the two men got to their feet.

'Just one more question' said Wainfield. 'Was the victim carrying anything with him, like a bag or folder?'

Paul thought about this question a moment.

'Yes Harry was carrying a bag' he said.

'What type of bag? Big, small? What colour?'

Paul thought hard. It seemed to him that Harry had had a brownish coloured bag with him as he walked with Paul down the street.

'Brown. Light brown. But the exact size I don't recall.'

Wainfield looked at him patiently and noted it down. They left the interview room and Paul was accompanied to the elevator bank. The hallway was filled with people coming and going, prisoners in handcuffs, undercover agents, uniformed cops.

On the way down in the elevator, Paul thought about this last remark. Now it came back to him. He had asked Harry Red when they met at Harry's house if he was going somewhere. The brown bag must be missing. Otherwise, why ask the question?

People had appeared at the scene in a matter of minutes, so whoever had shot Harry must also have taken the bag.

Which raised the question - what had been in it? Whatever it was, it was presumably the reason Harry Red had been shot. The contents of the bag must be important enough for someone to be prepared to strike in broad daylight, even with Paul there.

He got out of the elevator and went in search for a cab.

From the moment he had got to No. 1 Police Plaza, two men had been watching him. They now followed him outside the building and turned left, going down the steps. The dark blue Lexus was approaching the kerb. The men got in, the one in the front passenger seat reaching for a cellphone. The conversation was brief and in Spanish.

The Lexus picked up speed to follow Paul's cab midtown.

The next day a meeting took place in the midtown house owned by La Unidad. Two of the men present were of South American origin, the other three American. One of the South Americans gave the rest a progress report on the shadowing of Paul Anfield and the termination of Harry Red. Most of the time was spent discussing the file kept by the lawyer Lenny Gerstner. The time had come to remove it from the hands of his nephew. It had also been seen by the senior partner of Gerstner's firm.

Analysis was undertaken, conclusions weighed and finally orders given to the South Americans. When the meeting ended, the three Americans left through the kitchen door, crossed the small garden and were escorted outside, where immediately two cars pulled up, both with blacked-out windows. If someone had checked the licence plates, they would have found that the cars were registered to a special State Department detail. In the first car an angry John Cushing was muttering to the man sitting beside him, the Republican representative for Texas, the right honourable Senator Marcus Wellington the Third, well known in Washington and internationally acknowledged as the Chairman of the International Security Board, the much more powerful replacement for the Inter-America Security Committee.

Marcus Wellington was used to Cushing's sudden fits. Not that he had anything in common with Cushing, nor did he have the least interest in him. Cushing served the Marcus Wellingtons of the world. They took care of 'wet work' – killing people. All the dirty business which every US President promised that the CIA and the rest would not be allowed to do on his watch.

People like Cushing were simply hidden more carefully, their actions always well removed from any direct government link.

In the past 40 years the US government had spend an enormous amount of time and money taking care that 'Oliver North situations' would become a thing of the past, a lesson learned. But the game, the rules, the enemies, were always evolving. The Cushings of this world came with democracy - they were democracy, they carried democracy, but in reality they were just professionals with a mission. Their mission was the USA.

'Why did that bloody idiot keep a file? Why?' said Cushing. He meant, of course, Lenny Gerstner. Wellington didn't answer. They drove in silence for a few blocks.

'Now listen' said Wellington. 'Our friends will take care of the nephew, so we need to concentrate on the managing partner. What do we have on him or his firm?'

Cushing took out a file from the seat beside him. He had already studied this part, knowing perfectly well how men like Wellington always reacted. Mind over matter. No rash decisions, just carefully-elaborated plans to defuse any situation, anywhere.

'Lewman, Applebaum and Fromm started doing the Kaneko transaction in 1970. We chose Gerstner through his relationship with your predecessor, Senator Peter Brooks.' Cushing went through the file. Wellington already knew these details; he had studied them time and again during the past week. It had given him time to ponder what to do.

He had also found out about the relationship between Gerstner and Peter Brooks. Brooks had served on the China Commission at the end of the 1960s. The China Commission was a typical Bobby Kennedy invention, and a result of the Allen Dulles school of thought – special secret commissions containing top-ranking officials from the State Department, the military, the FBI and the CIA. All with the same line: stop communist influence spilling over. Now, more than 20 years later, practically all the covert actions and activities had been written about and documented and people had been called on to justify the deeds they had done for their political leaders.

However a fair number of these initiatives had never become known to anybody, least of all the public. The China Commission was one of these. Funds for these operations came from unknown sources, but one of them was the drugs trade, led by a whole army of CIA people or those closely related to the Agency. This became known later, but no-one knew just how much money it generated. Very few in government knew even the rough figures coming out of the government-sponsored drug trade, supposedly serving the greater good of safeguarding the USA.

Cushing shifted in his seat, straining the seams of the blue polyester suit, so typical of the ex-military. The traffic heading midtown was getting heavier.

It was through the drugs trade in South East Asia that the connection was made between the US government, represented by a young Peter Brooks on his way up in politics, and a young lawyer named Lenny Gerstner.

Wellington thought about the note he had read. Brooks and Gerstner had met in Saigon by accident. Brooks had been there to talk with a number of South Vietnamese generals who were actively involved in the drugs trade for the Americans. The meetings with generals took place outside Saigon, in a specially-protected compound.

Washington was increasingly sure that North Vietnam would win the war, but that everything should in the meantime be done to delay it.

At the meetings the generals also introduced to Brooks an Italian business partner: Alessandro Caruna, the youngest of the Caruna clan and direct family, as Brooks later found out, of Robert Anfield, Gerstner's brother-in-law. The South Vietnamese generals had a 'transportation' arrangement with Caruna. Brooks and others knew perfectly well that the generals were regularly shipping out all kinds of personal possessions to Hong Kong and further afield. The transport planes handled by the Italian also had the protection they needed to make all kinds of pickups of drugs in neighbouring areas.

Later on that sticky Saigon night, Peter Brooks had driven back in the same car as Alessandro Caruna. Fate even placed them in the same hotel. Upon reaching the hotel, Alessandro invited Brooks for a last beer in the bar on the top floor.

Alessandro Caruna was the youngest brother, and a modern professional drugs operator who was technically ahead of his time. Later it was proved that the Italians were the first ones to use the coffins of US soldiers by packing them with drugs before they were flown home. Alessandro spoke fluent English, French and German and was a great sportsman, in contrast to his oldest brother Giuseppe, the family and clan leader, known for his ready use of extreme violence.

They were joined at the bar by Lenny Gerstner, who had just arrived from Paris and was in Saigon to help his client, Alessandro, with a number of US government contracts for Caruna companies in South East Asia. Brooks had of course smelled the real relationship between the Vietnamese generals and Alessandro, but in that first meeting it appeared to him that Gerstner was an authentic lawyer, acting on behalf of a client. Brooks already knew that Gerstner was highly regarded by the State Department, thanks to services rendered.

The three men all got on so well that the next day Brooks asked Washington to do a full background check on Alessandro Caruna, his activities and his lawyer Gerstner. The information that he got back was stellar. They were highly appreciated people, and it was one's duty to help them when requested. If Washington knew what Caruna's real activities were, this was not deemed relevant. It was off limits for people like him.

So Peter Brooks and Lenny Gerstner became close over the years following Vietnam. It was not a friendship but a relationship based on mutual professional respect and the knowledge of how to get things fixed in Washington. Perhaps their differences in character and as human beings made the relationship easier; Peter Brooks had only one objective in life, his own glory and success. The things all politicians need to become successful.

Gerstner, however, was a man driven by decency and principal. That was a weakness while he was on the way up towards becoming the ultimate successful New York corporate lawyer.

Peter Brooks then died, relatively young, around his 60th birthday. By then he was already working very closely with the up-and-coming Marcus Wellington, soon to be one of the youngest senators in US history. Through Brooks, Wellington also became acquainted with Lenny Gerstner. He was a board member on several major companies which were corporate clients of Lewman, Applebaum and Fromm.

Wellington had quickly detected Gerstner's basic human and professional decency. He had always wondered when the lawyer would finally understand the inescapable trap he had entered so many years back, when he had entered the world created by Peter Brooks and the Liskers. It was only a matter of time.

The car was slowly advancing, traffic still at a crawl. Cushing ordered the driver to head for Roosevelt Boulevard. Wellington had still said nothing.

Cushing had stopped fuming and had closed the file and put it on his lap. Wellington looked at it. So what had triggered Gerstner to start this paper trail?

Wellington tuned his head and spoke. 'I want Anfield checked out. Everything.   His office, his house, all his files, computers, telephones.'

Cushing didn't react at first. Then after a few minutes he flipped upon his phone, punched a number and passed on Wellington's instructions.

The traffic was no better when the car turned on to F D Roosevelt.

CHAPTER 19

Madrid 1991

'I'm sorry but we need to sell our shares, Mr Diaz. I do appreciate your reasons for suggesting the contrary, but the present turmoil will only get worse. Our board has been in hourly contact with us and these are its requirements. We will ask our brokers to instruct our bankers to unwind our positions from the start of business tomorrow, 0900 hours New York time.'

The voice of the man from Deutsche Wert Bank in Frankfurt came clearly through the speaker box on Ramon Diaz' desk in his Madrid office. They had been on the phone for more than an hour, while Diaz tried to persuade the CEO of one of Germany largest institutional investors and a 4% Virtuvio shareholder to change his mind about selling his holding back into the market.

Beside Diaz' desk was a TV set with the sound switched off, tuned to CNN. They were still reporting on a war which seemed to be running according to the station's own whims, just to make sure the world stayed glued to it.

The equity markets worldwide were continuing to drop by the day and since the start of the Gulf War the Virtuvio shares had lost more than 45%. The Virtuvio market maker, responsible for keeping an orderly market in the shares, had practically given up. The orders to sell kept on coming, and no buyers could be found.

During the first few weeks Diaz had orchestrated buying efforts with a number of friendly banks, investors and brokers, but the flow and sliding stock price made it a futile effort. BANINSA of course was going the same way, thanks to its relationship with Virtuvio.

Diaz sighed and turned back to the speaker.

'Well thank you anyhow for attending this conference call, Dr Herzog. Please be advised that our friends at Rheinman will keep you informed of developments.'

The call ended. Diaz wondered what to do next. Every day he was on the phone or in meetings trying to persuade investors not to sell Virtuvio shares but to buy more.

His secretary called on the other line; the Rheinman people in London wanted to go over the conference call with Germany. Like good, disciplined investment bankers they were staying close to their paying client – Diaz - even though they knew that trying to place shares in such a market was a futile exercise.

Diaz knew that the market had reached the point where three answers were possible: one was 'no, I don't have money or access to it', the second was 'yes, I have cash and access to liquidity' and the third, connected to the second, was 'But why should I buy now if in three to six months I'll get it for half the price?'

It was clearly a 'falling dagger' market - trying to make a trade in these conditions was like trying to catch a falling knife.

His secretary called. 'Mr de Ronin's secretary is inviting you for lunch or dinner, today' she said. 'I told her you were booked for lunch with the Canadian people and tonight with the Fondo Vida people.'

The Canadian Caisse de Montreal et Québec, a very large investor in international equity on behalf of their customers and clients, were in town and had been studying the possibility of investing in Virtuvio, but the present market conditions had ensured that the meetings had dragged on.

Today Diaz had hoped to try to strike a deal. Or not. And tonight he was supposed to be having dinner with Spain's largest pension fund,

Fondo Vida, belonging to Spain's national telephone company.

But Emilio de Ronin didn't 'invite' you for lunch or dinner. It was more like an order.

Who to choose – the Canadians or Fondo Vida?

'Suzanna' he said. 'Call Mr de Ronin's office and tell them we'll see each for dinner. Tell Sanchez of the change of plan for tonight.' He rang off.

Having dinner with de Ronin, 99 times out of 100, meant going to his house in Somosaguas, an exclusive enclave east of Madrid. Emilio de Ronin never went to public places like restaurants. The only exception was on behalf of his wife Rafaela, who was a recognized patron of Spain's music scene.

Diaz' team had all left the room. He got up and walked to the main window of his office. It was on the top floor of a medium-sized office building, giving him a clear view of Serrano, Madrid's prime shopping street. The weather was beautiful, and Serrano was filled with shoppers. But Diaz was thinking only of what de Ronin would be putting forward tonight. The economic situation of the Virtuvio group was a healthy one - the net cash the various group companies jointly produced was enough to service both individual and group debt. This was the only thing that mattered to the Banco del Norte y Cantabria and its President and controlling shareholder, Emilio de Ronin.

Banco del Norte y Cantabria were not interested in capital market operations like the ones Diaz and his partners were mounting with Rheinman and similar capital providers. No, they were old fashioned: they borrowed money, they got a spread and you paid back the money including the spread. If that worked you didn't have a problem. If it didn't, they were going to be all over you, and then Spain suddenly became a suffocatingly small market.

The de Ronin family had been making money that way for three generations, and they were not going to change now. In spite of Diaz' presence.

Diaz and his entourage arrived at Emilio de Ronin's house at 10 o'clock that night. The house was a perfect reflection of its owner – sober but imposing. Cold, but stylish. Discreet, but with the elegance of thoughtful design. The house was well protected, both by security and the lush greenery around it, which made it practically impossible for paparazzi to shoot photos of it or the people living there or visiting.

Diaz was shown into a large study, where he was offered a drink; he settled for mineral water. The study seemed surprisingly cosy, which struck him as odd. It had sofas and two very large mahogany tables which were overflowing with a mixture of papers, files, magazines and books. In the centre was a half-oval desk with more papers and two large telephone consoles. The lighting was restrained, the room white with burgundy shades on the lamps.

Everywhere there were photos of de Ronin. Not the usual pictures showing the head of the household with famous or important people; they were all family related. Diaz thought this must be an inner sanctum, the secluded and private place where de Ronin met with people he wanted to talk to very privately.

'Como estas?' De Ronin walked towards Ramon with his outstretched hand, indicating with his other hand that he should take a seat at the half-oval desk. A butler had already brought some mineral water, plus a bottle of beer for de Ronin.

They discussed the markets and the impact of the Gulf War on the world economy. Finally de Ronin raised the main subject of their meeting.

'Ramon, I called you tonight on behalf of the Banco de España. They are worried that your fundraising will not close on time. The markets are drying up due to this Gulf War and local institutional support for your project is not likely. If your Virtuvio offering doesn't attract the right level of funding, its potential default size is a risk for the entire Spanish economy.

'I have a proposal, but it needs an answer from you here and now, in this house, tonight.'

He handed Diaz a paper. Diaz knew the BANINSA situation was getting desperate. The money from the Virtuvio IPO and the proceeds of the Iberia de Quimica had been invested in a string of companies, including the controlling stake they had bought in BANINSA. All investments they had made through Virtuvio were suffering and it was impossible to raise cash through asset sales. Rheinman was working against the clock to prepare a major investment from one of its own funds to inject liquidity into BANINSA.

On top of this, it was a poorly-kept secret that Diaz had borrowed heavily to purchase additional BANINSA shares for his own account. The loan had come from a small regional bank which was run by de Ronin's younger brother Raul.

Diaz had become an isolated man within the Spanish business establishment. His meteoric ascent had made a lot of powerful people nervous. When these established powerhouses became agitated, the first thing they did was to align themselves with political power. In this case, Diaz had antagonized both the socialists and the opposition. Left and right had both decided that Diaz sooner or later would try to make a break towards political power, and that was a no-go. He had sealed his fate by also investing in radio and TV stations and publishers, through both BANINSA and Virtuvio.

It was clear that he was isolated. Preparations were clearly being made to squeeze him out of the Spanish power picture.

Diaz read the one-page document. It was written on plain white paper with no name, address or other details. It contained a list of required steps and subsequent resulting actions.

Basically there were four steps, starting with him stepping down from all executive roles at all the companies he and/or Virtuvio controlled. The second step would be to sell his personal share holding in BANINSA to a consortium of local banks and the Central Bank through a special guarantee fund. The third step was similar to the second, but concerned the investments in radio, TV and publishing. A number of well-known local players were earmarked as buyers for these assets.

The fourth step was an unspecified price offering for his 50% Virtuvio stake, according to prevailing market conditions.

The note continued that these steps and the resulting actions were to be non-negotiable. Diaz was going to be 'retired' with sufficient money for his needs, his projects liquidated and taken over. All parties were acting to ensure that Spain and the Spanish public were not going to suffer any damage.

What didn't need to be explained or written down was what would happen if Diaz refused to sign tonight. He would simply be crushed by the judicial system. The courts were ultimately controlled by the political powers, who had a rich history of influencing and shaping through the outcomes of public matters and issues through the judicial process.

Diaz pushed the paper back to de Ronin. De Ronin looked him in the eye, saying nothing.

This was ridiculous! This was Spain, part of Europe – and yet an orchestrated coup was being executed under the direct supervision of the political powers, jointly with a group of established Spanish power brokers and with the explicit support of its Central Bank.

Diaz knew there was nothing he could do. Just the same, he made sure that his expression revealed nothing to de Ronin.

He got up and walked towards a window which gave a view over a lighted garden and swimming pool beyond.

'Who?'

'You know who.'

'Why are they so afraid?'

De Ronin said nothing. He got to his feet and walked over to one of the telephone consoles, picked up a line and speed-dialled a number. Over the speakerphone Ramon could hear a familiar voice; de Ronin's brother Raul.

'Hola Raul. Estoy aqui con Ramon' said de Ronin. 'I have made him aware of the situation and given him the suggestions in writing so that we can find a mutual acceptable solution.'

'Ramon' came the metallic voice of Raul. 'Let me first say that I am sorry that matters have reached this stage. I was called some days ago by Banco de España. They told me they were going to prepare administrative executive action in view of the risk of the combined BANINSA-Virtuvio situation to the stability of the system.'

Diaz said nothing, so Raul de Ronin continued.

'Please understand that I conveyed to them my disagreement with the steps being proposed. Your personal financial obligations were and always have been met by you, so I made it very clear that no change would come to your standing and financial credibility at our bank.'

At least one gentleman is not yet sticking the knife in me, thought Diaz. If this had been his brother, Emilio, matters would have been very different.

Raul de Ronin continued to explain how the pressure had been building up via a variety of parties. Diaz knew this already, but had not been in a position to put up a defence, or anything like one.

What options were left? His personal financial situation was going to be hit severely as soon as he signed the document. Virtuvio would lose even further share value, on top of the 45% fall since the IPO. Worse still, his partners Lisker and Cantarini would lose practically all the money they had invested in Virtuvio. Along with all the friends and family members they had involved in the situation.

Diaz focused again on the voice at the other end of the speakerphone.

'If I can say this as a friend, Ramon – take the offer. I know, I know: it is unspeakable what is being presented, but you knew this could happen.' Raul de Ronin waited for Diaz' reaction. Diaz looked into Emilio de Ronin's dark eyes. He saw no flicker of sympathy. De Ronin looked like a lion surveying a kill which had just been carried out by the rest of his pride.

Ramon Diaz knew that a man like Emilio de Ronin would always be at the top of the food chain, especially with prey of the calibre of BANINSA. For de Ronin and his Banco del Norte y Cantabria to swallow even part of BANINSA would make it the undisputed leader in financial services in Spain.

'Gracias, Raul' said Ramon. 'I'll talk it over further now with Emilio and we'll let you know one way or the other'. The brothers said goodbye and Emilio disconnected the call.

Silence.

Ramon sat down again at the oval table.

'Would you like to have some time alone?'

'No thank you Emilio. We had better get this over with. It doesn't make sense to keep on fighting. I presume the note was drafted by the Secretary?' He meant the Secretary of the Banco de España.

They both knew that the note came from a coalition of adversaries who did not have the guts to tackle Diaz alone. Some of them were men he had brought to their knees on his way up.

Diaz also knew that his separation from Pedro Cortes had come to hound him. At the end of the day, when his 'protection' fell away, Ramon Diaz became an intruder in a club where no membership rules existed. If you expected rules, you had come to the wrong place.

Emilio de Ronin still waited patiently, not moving, the paper still on the table.

'What happens now?' said Diaz

'If you agree, I will give you the original on Banco de España paper. When you have signed we'll call Moreno. He is waiting at the bank. We'll set up a meeting tomorrow at eight o'clock at their offices. They will draft a note for the Stock Exchange and the press. After the phone call you'd better tell your key people at BANINSA that from midday tomorrow, new management is taking over.'

Everything had been foreseen; everything had been carefully planned and orchestrated. As you would expect. You don't bring in one of the largest banks and groups in the country without using military precision. And Juan Moreno, the carefully chosen President of the Banco de España and an intimate friend of the socialist political establishment, had no margin for error in the exercise of closing Diaz down. He still was one of Spain's most prominent people and a real power to be accounted for. The intervention of BANINSA, the dismantling of Virtuvio and the stepping down of Ramon Diaz would be front-page news for some time to come.

Diaz drew a pen from inside his jacket, took hold of the paper, read it one more time and asked de Ronin for the original. He read it. The language was formal and differed from the draft, but it said the same thing with longer words.

He signed.

'Let's make the call' said Diaz.

Ramon Diaz had just signed away everything he had fought so hard for. And still Emilio de Ronin showed no reaction, no movement.

De Ronin stood up and speed-dialled the number of the Banco de España. BANINSA was to be moved back into the hands of those who had originally controlled it - the Spanish power class. Diaz would be stripped of all the power he had built up. Within a few years he would be indicted, together with a number of his close associates, for theft of BANINSA shareholders' funds and related matters. Whether the accusations were real or invented didn't really matter. Ramon Diaz was out. He had played the game against the Spanish establishment and lost.

Emilio de Ronin would eventually gain control over BANINSA, and the old balance of power would be re-established.

CHAPTER 20

New York

'Paul, I really think you should take a break. The partners are getting increasingly nervous about this Kaneko business, your uncle's role and the position of the office.'

David Fromm had been talking to Paul Anfield for more than 45 minutes, since the moment they had sat down for lunch at the top of the Pan Am building, as everyone still called it, although the name had been changed years before.

Fromm had always been a member of the club, and usually did his internal PR and other office-related businesses there. Typical of David, it was relatively cheap and not a place to take clients to. It had gained the reputation among his colleagues and friends as one of the worst places in town to eat. The food was consistently appalling.

Lewmans' managing partner was on edge. Tension had been running high since the moment, just after the partners had discussed the Kaneko file for the first time, when the people from the Department of State had suddenly appeared. They had arrived unannounced, asked for David Fromm, showed their credentials and introduced themselves without further preamble as the legitimate owners of Mercado Libre Ltd and all the associated companies that had been handled by Lenny Gerstner over the years. Fromm had called in two other senior partners who had had dealings with the Washington culture.

The meeting had lasted 60 minutes. The three partners had come away with a very clear message - all documents regarding Kaneko which might still be on the premises were to be handed over immediately to the leading Washington law firm of Clayborn Ackerman, who were famous for the work they did on behalf of the Ministry of Defence and the State Department.

Lewmans were also asked to immediately submit a final invoice for work done and any outstanding work in connection with Mercado Libre. They were promised an additional payment of one million dollars to cover future losses of potential revenue.

The visitors left a very clearly-worded document, which was to be signed by the four members of Lewmans' partners management committee. It stated that all dealings concerning Kaneko and Mercado Libre were, as of now, state classified documents and carried the usual responsibilities and threats of jail sentences.

There were no niceties, no courtesies. David Fromm and his partners had been openly and blatantly threatened.

Fromm's partners were outraged. The moment the men from the government had gone, they hit the phones to their Washington contacts. They were not offered help, but advised to cooperate.

Less than an hour later, David Fromm received a call on his private cellphone from John Clayborn, founder and managing partner of Clayborn Ackerman. David knew of John Clayborn, but only then did he discover just how much power he wielded.

Clayborn, as one lawyer to another, had made a few suggestions. He had made it clear on behalf of his 'client' that David and his partners had just one week to prepare everything for an orderly turnover of the requested material, along with the signed document. He had ended the conversation by warning Fromm not to make any further enquiries within Washington. If any Lewman partner needed to talk, he should phone Clayborn direct.

This was the reason for David Fromm's anger and frustration during his lunch with Paul, who had no difficulty in understanding the depth of anger David was feeling. He had never in his personal or professional life been treated this way. Clients were supposed to follow instructions, and to pay top dollar for them.

Paul said he would think about his response to the ultimatum.

'No Paul' said Fromm. 'We as a partnership can't afford to give any impression that we are resisting. Clayborn was utterly clear. We are not talking about a client relationship. The US Government is ready to bury us as a firm, as a partnership!'

People at tables nearby looked up when they heard his tone. An angry David Fromm was not something they had seen at the club before.

'How can I help the partnership?' said Paul.

'Take some leave. Stay away for a while, make a trip.'

Anfield didn't know what to say. The whole business of his Uncle Lenny and what he had been up to was clearly eating away at David Fromm.

'OK' he said. 'After lunch I'll go through my files with my team and see who can handle the most urgent ones. Then I'll go for a break somewhere.'

'Good, that's settled. I'll tell the rest of the office that you'll be doing some travelling' said Fromm, relieved.

They ordered coffee.

Some 20 minutes later, Anfield and Fromm left the Pan Am building on the Park Avenue side. The Lexus stood at the opposite kerb. One of the men was holding a camera with a long lens. As the two lawyers walked back to their offices, he took pictures.

By the time Paul Anfield had handed over his current caseload to his colleagues, internal rumours had already circulated to the effect that his sudden plan to take leave of absence had something to do with the heightened state of tension at partner level following Harry Red's death. Precise information was lacking. All Paul said was that he had to take care of a number of issues concerning the estate of his Uncle Lenny.

Somewhere near TriBeCa, Deborah White was finishing a document at her desk at a small publishing company. The company was a sleepy affair owned by an uncle of hers who had been kind enough to arrange somewhere to stay and work while she was in New York.

Deborah had realised that she was bored, and whenever she felt boredom coming on she set out to find something interesting to do. Life was too short to be bored, even for a second. Boredom was for other people. Her family money had given her the freedom to make sure of that.

So why not surprise Paul, pick up some sushi and take it to his fifth-floor loft on Bayard Street? It was near the corner with Baxter Street with its unique terrace overlooking Columbus Park. He always kept wine and champagne in his fridge, so she didn't need to worry about those.

She switched off her PC, said goodbye to the old office secretary (who liked her, but could never really understand her) and walked out of the office, down the stairs and into Walker Street.

At exactly the same moment, two men in overalls with the ATT logo on their backs just happened to enter Paul's apartment building. The caretaker, old Mr Ramirez, was a Cuban exile and his English was still very poor even after more than 35 years in New York. But that didn't matter, because the two men spoke Spanish. They showed him a document that said certain cable boxes near the top of the building needed to be re-set. Mr Ramirez looked at the familiar logos and motioned them to carry on without a second thought.

The two men were Hector 'Capitan Loco' Washington and Rufus 'El Muerte' Chanco, both from La Unidad. Washington was carrying what looked like a tool box. That morning they had received instructions to place cameras and microphones in the apartment on Bayard Street which belonged to the lawyer Paul Anfield. The men shadowing Paul had confirmed that he was safely at his office.

Hector Washington's nickname had been earned for extraordinary bravery while serving in the Colombian Army and combating the FRAC. He had once needed money to pay for a special heart operation for his youngest daughter. When he found out about the deals his commanders had arranged for themselves, he knew his future within the military was over.

To pay back the money for the operation, his commanders made him responsible for their drugs operations. So when he was invited to join La Unidad, it was an easy decision. His bosses didn't dare to come near him once they knew that he had joined La Unidad. They knew like so many that it would have meant the unavoidable death of his daughter.

Hector didn't really like working with El Muerte. He had a reputation for being almost a psychopath. In the Colombian Army Special Forces he had been known for unnecessary violence. His commanding officers had used him, as they had Washington, for their personal business. Especially in the case of people who hadn't paid up.

Calling in El Muerte was usually a very reliable way to make sure you got paid. Unfortunately, not many people survived his methods.

Chanco was also one of the army's best snipers. One day while off duty he had killed the wrong man. He had had to leave the army, and it was then he had been introduced to La Unidad.

As with Hector Washington, all Chanco's military history was wiped. Such was the influence of La Unidad.

The men reached the fifth floor and entered Anfield's apartment without difficulty. No burglar alarm had been installed. They went through the apartment, looked at its layout and decided where to install the microphones. Then they got to work.

They did not know about Deborah White and the surprise sushi delivery, and they did not hear the sound of the elevator travelling back downstairs to collect her from the ground floor.

When Deborah opened Paul's door with her spare key, she saw the back of a man in ATT overalls - Hector Washington, busy installing a small but very powerful microphone behind a painting in the living room. She paused in shock.

Chanco, in the kitchen, heard the door to the apartment open, and came through to see what was going on. Deborah did not have a chance to ask what the men were doing in Paul's apartment. As she swung round to look at the second man, 'El Muerte' took out his silenced Heckler & Koch and before she could speak, in one smooth movement, he shot her between the eyes.

Hector Washington would have preferred to try to talk their way out of it, but he knew as well as Chanco that the woman who had suddenly entered the apartment was a serious security hazard.

Deborah fell backwards, the bags of food cascading over the floor. Blood began to ooze from the hole in her face.

Chanco stepped over Deborah's body, closed the front door and removed Deborah's key from her limp fingers. Hector Washington got out his phone.

'Tenemos una complicacion. The girlfriend walked in. We had to react.' He looked down at Deborah, listened for his instructions and closed the phone.

The instructions were clear – clean up any fingerprints, remove any other evidence and leave, quickly.

When the two men had done as ordered, they changed out of their overalls and left the apartment. Downstairs, old Mr Ramirez had dozed off. Nobody took any notice of the two neatly-dressed men as they got into their car and drove off.

Paul appeared 45 minutes later. He did not see the Lexus waiting opposite.

He entered his apartment to receive the biggest shock of his life.

Twice in a few days he had seen violent death, and this time it was a young and beautiful woman and someone he had been very close to. He held her in his arms for a few moments before gathering himself together.

Paul gathered himself together, went to his phone, dialled 911 and told the police what had happened. Just before he rang off he remembered to ask them to inform Detective Wainfield, the man he had spoken to after Harry's murder. Then he slumped on to the floor, gazing again in disbelief at Deborah's beautiful dead body.

Neither Hector Washington nor Rufus Chanco had noticed when they had entered Paul Anfield's building that on the other side of the road stood a black Jeep Cherokee with tinted windows. Neither had the two men inside, who were following orders from John Cushing, thought anything of the two men in ATT overalls. The men sent by Cushing had only one task - watching Anfield. Under no circumstances was any engagement to be sought. They had seen and photographed Deborah as she arrived, and then done the same with Paul Anfield. That was all. So when suddenly police cruisers appeared with their sirens and blue lights on, they had a surprise. The surprise became bigger when the police started to enter Anfield's building. The men in the Cherokee decided to wait, while on the pavement people started to gather.

More police cars arrived, including undercover cars and an ambulance. Once a good crowd had gathered, one of the men left the

Cherokee and walked over to the apartment building. Then he returned to the car. He already had a phone in his hand and had been speed-dialling a number.

'Yes?'

'This is 21. Connect me with Central.'

A few seconds later, Cushing came on the line.

'It's 21. A girl has been killed in the subject's apartment. We presume it's the girlfriend. We have photos of her arriving.'

'Did you see anything?'

'Nothing out of the ordinary.'

'Stay with the subject' said Cushing.

Somewhere in a midtown office tower, John Cushing sat back. First the lawyer's assistant had been terminated, now his girlfriend. And nobody had seen anything. Delving into New York Metropolitan databases and people on the inside had brought up nothing either.

The call by 21 Unit, part of DSA, the Defense Security Agency, only confirmed Cushing's and Wellington's suspicion – that somebody else had woken up to the appearance of the documents assembled by the dead lawyer.

Cushing got up from his desk and walked out of the room. He passed a large central operating room, manned with people staring at screens, and turned towards the bank of elevators. This was the monitoring centre for a number of states. Cushing had split the USA into a number of key areas, monitoring phone conversations, email traffic and any other traceable communications by people who were interested in them.

Wellington had got funds from a variety of sources to run their activities, which were a crossover between State, CIA, FBI, NSA and other security agencies. He had secured total independence. As far as Cushing knew, Wellington reported to a committee whose members never met in person, only through secure video conferencing. They were untraceable.

In addition, a number of government security industries were in the habit of making 'contributions' – special gifts to a number of causes which were closely controlled by Wellington and his committee.

Only Wellington was a permanent member of the committee. Everyone else took turns every four years, ensuring fresh ideas and support. Members were carefully chosen. Everyone serving on the committee knew that its purpose was first and foremost to provide instant solutions to covert operations by any branch of the United States Government.

The DSA had been set up during the Vietnam war, when it had become clear to US political and military leadership that the conflict had moved across the border. Laos and Cambodia were effectively supporting North Vietnam and the Vietcong, though they were not involved in conflict with the USA.

A solution was found, supported by Lyndon Johnson's mainly Texas-based defence contractors. Over the years Wellington had built a magnificent off-the-radar 'clean-up' agency, utterly separated from the US Government and its funding. Wellington and the DSA backers had a very clear view – democracy could only lead over time to closer public scrutiny over how conflicts were run and at what price in the lives of US soldiers.

The deceased lawyer had been vital in organising matters in Central and South America in the past. Most importantly, he had been handpicked by Marcus Wellington. Cushing therefore knew that the matter needed to be treated with the greatest care.

But then it occurred to him that perhaps the others, whoever they were, who had been awoken by these events would clean up certain parts of the mess themselves.

CHAPTER TWENTY

Damage control on their side – for and on behalf of the always-overriding interest of the Government – would be focused on the dead lawyer's firm. This had already been initiated by John Clayborn at Clayborn Ackerman. Clayborn had been a committee member and was still a trusted ally of Wellington.

Cushing said goodbye to the people securing the entrance of the floors they occupied and went down in one of the elevators, followed by his bodyguards.

CHAPTER 21

Detective Wainfield arrived about 20 minutes after the rest of the police. He led Paul away from the officers who were questioning him and they went outside, where forensics had already started their traces investigation.

Other police officers were trying to get information out of Mr Ramirez, who was clearly in shock and could only blabber in Spanish.

In the hall leading to his apartment, Wainfield asked Paul to go over his story again.

'I left my office about 50 minutes ago. I came by cab. I went up to my apartment and found her' Paul answered, in a flat voice.

Wainfield already knew through the coroner's people that Deborah had been dead for no more than an hour. He knew instinctively that Paul was not a killer. But for Wainfield that was just the problem. If he wasn't a killer, why in such a short time span would the same man be present at the scenes of two murders?

'You're connected directly to both the victims' he said. 'Help me try to understand this. Did something happen lately that could have provoked all this? Are you working on something, a case, whatever – representing certain criminals? Why do fake service repairmen burgle your apartment and disappear without a trace after getting disturbed in the act by a girlfriend of yours? Why did they kill her?'

Paul didn't immediately respond, but he now knew for sure that it was the Kaneko file. Nothing else could have triggered the events of the last few days. But the file under no circumstances could be shown to nosy police investigators. There was a real risk that the material could be leaked to the press.

Paul immediately and instinctively knew one thing – certain people who had been intimately connected with his uncle's past were on full alert. And they were determined to make sure the Kaneko file would never see the light of day.

Wainfield, being the experienced cop he was, sensed a change in Paul's body language.

'You have something to tell me?'

'No. Nothing. I can't imagine what it could be. My firm is only involved in commercial work – we've never handled private matters. No divorces or anything, certainly no drug dealers. If anything like that comes up we refer them to another firm. We are commercial lawyers.' He was trying to make it clear that he was not going to be pushed around.

'I didn't say drug dealers. You said drug dealers. Why?'

'Neither drug dealing nor any criminal ventures. Clear, Mr Wainfield?' Paul answered back.

Wainfield kept on asking questions and Paul kept deflecting them. All the time he was working out how he could get away as quickly as possible, without irritating Wainfield.

He was allowed to leave about 10 minutes later. As he left, the ambulance people were carrying down Deborah's body. The sight of the stretcher made him even more focused on the situation at hand. He now had a clear idea of what he wanted to achieve – to get in contact one way or the other with these people who were so obsessed with making sure the Kaneko file and its contents were not going to be spilled.

He left the building, walked through the crowd and waved down a passing cab. The Cherokee on the opposite kerb started its engine and started to follow.

When he arrived at his office, he collected his laptop and some files and went straight up to the floor where the firm's library was located. It was empty apart from some juniors slugging away at data gathering.

After an hour, he had managed to lift from the Kaneko file and his previous notes a short list of names, events, leads and facts. He then drew lines through them, connecting them into a rough diagram. All the points connected to other points, based on the data. Then he tried to connect facts and names. Circles within circles.

Finally he had two circles that were connected to a common core. They represented on one side the US Government and on the other hand a man called Felipe Lisker. The other name he found was a man who had remained hidden throughout: Marcus Wellington.

Paul switched screens on his PC, googled both the names and started to read. After a little digging, a pattern started to become clear.

Both Marcus Wellington and Felipe Lisker had come a long way. Over these last 30 or so years, Wellington had become a Washington fixture where everything related to the defence industry was concerned. Lisker had become a respected international industrialist, but had left no clues to the origin of his wealth. Basically, he was a Colombian coffee grower who had hit it rich - or that was how he wanted it to look.

Through Kaneko, both men had shared the same 'architect' in creating their future and present – his Uncle Lenny.

Paul went back to Google to start try to find an office number for Marcus Wellington. After some digging, he found a company name which appeared to be connected to Wellington. A few minutes later he was being put through to a defence-related lobby office somewhere in Washington.

No, Mr. Wellington was travelling and no, they didn't know when he would be back, but if he would care to leave a name, telephone number and message, he would be called back.

Paul gave his details, hung up and sat back. Soon, perhaps, his suspicions would be proved right.

Cushing was given Paul's number less than three minutes later. Immediately he called Wellington.

'The cousin called one of your numbers. He wants to speak to you.'

'Where is he now?'

'At his NY offices'

'Give me his cell number.'

Paul's phone rang; no ID was displayed.

'Mr Paul Anfield?'

'Mr Marcus Wellington, I presume?' Anfield answered promptly.

'My condolences over the loss of your uncle. You will be aware by now that your uncle and I shared a very long personal relationship.'

And don't forget the professional one, Paul thought.

'Mr. Anfield, I understand you have become aware that your uncle kept, er, a written reflection of the ventures we collaborated in over the years?'

What you are saying, Wellington, you slick Washington bastard, is that my uncle, for whatever reason, saw it necessary to document all ventures.

'Mr. Anfield? Are you still there?'

'Please do continue, Mr. Wellington'

'Well – as I said. I presume you have had time to reflect on the scope of the content of the notes in your possession. The written reflections by your uncle have, as you perhaps can appreciate, a rather delicate nature. Therefore...'

'I fully subscribe to your observations, Mr Wellington, which is why of course we will bring this to the immediate attention of the State

Attorney's office and perhaps the press' Paul continued, without letting Wellington finish.

Wellington didn't miss a beat. He went on: 'Perhaps it would be worth our while to explore mutually how to proceed?'

'Explore mutually how to proceed? Sorry Mr Wellington, but I am lost there. The role fulfilled by yourself, as described by my uncle in these documents, makes you an instigator and accomplice in an uncountable number of crimes. With or without the explicit consent of the US Congress and our President.'

Wellington was very far from beaten.

'All the more reason to jointly evaluate any next steps! The events described are of clear national security interest and should be treated as such.'

'I still don't understand where this is leading us' Paul countered. 'I hope you are not expecting me to entertain any sort of negotiations as what to do with the blatantly clear documents on my table?'

Wellington let out a small chuckle.

'Mr Anfield, for the sake of the very long friendship I enjoyed with your uncle, would you allow me at least half an hour of your time?' Wellington must realise he needed to meet Paul in person to deal with this.

Paul had been waiting for this one.

'Why should that be necessary, Mr. Wellington? I mean – the documented activities and initiatives by a number of people, their undeniable relationship in one way or another with the Government, are very clear. What would a personal meeting add to this?'

Again Wellington side-stepped Paul.

'At face value, nobody could object to your observation about the documents you have seen. But that wouldn't be taking into account the very personal and direct relationship your uncle enjoyed with regard to the issues described. That relationship obliges me to defend your uncle's acts. If these documents get out of a contained government environment, I don't know what might happen.'

Paul got the point. 'Such as - violent death?'

'Excuse me?'

'The deaths of both a person who worked all his life close to my uncle and a close friend of mine.'

'I'm sorry Mr. Anfield, I don't know what you are talking about. However, if you feel these unfortunate events are connected to the file in your possession then I would suggest it is an even more compelling reason to meet at your earliest convenience.'

'I'm sorry Mr. Wellington, but I don't think we have anything further to discuss, or any reason to meet in person.'

'Then thank you for your time, Mr. Anfield' Wellington replied after a short pause. 'I know that you are now even more aware of the extremely sensitive nature of the documents in your possession. Do let me know if you change your mind. Goodbye'

Paul closed his phone. He knew now he had confirmed one point: some very shadowy political fixer with a life in US politics and defence-related matters behind him was determined not to let the Kaneko file become public knowledge.

What would they do to stop the information in the file getting out? How long before they acted? If these last few days were anything to go by, Paul had to move quickly, if only to protect his own life and those of others related to him.

He took the elevator down to his office and began scanning the file and his notes again. Then he saved them on a data stick. The originals he put in a file for internal mail back to David Fromm. In fact he had no doubt that the file would soon disappear - either officially or unofficially.

He shredded his notes. Then he went one last time through his emails, forwarding the relevant ones to his office team and secretary.

One email caught his attention. The front desk had just sent a message that during his absence a certain Carolina Monterey had called. She had left a mobile number, which Paul punched into his Nokia. Then he closed his laptop and put it into his Hartmann briefcase.

CHAPTER 22

In the cab, Paul made a series of calls. First he spoke to Detective Wainfield to request permission to get some clothes from his apartment. Wainfield said he would inform the people on guard that he would be coming by. Naturally an officer would have to be present when he did his packing.

Then he called his younger brother Mario, who worked as a client representative at Goal One, one of the world's largest agencies for sports people. Mario was three years younger than Paul, but the brothers had always had a very close relationship. Goal One's founder had been a corporate client with Paul. One day while Mario had been slogging through his first year's training at Goldman Sachs on Wall Street, he had confessed to his brother that banking would not be his future, in any form. He wanted to do something connected with his life interest – sports.

Mario had twice been a USA Student Championship tennis finalist and had started playing satellite tournaments, but a recurring knee problem had obliged him to come back to 'normal' life, as he described it. After finishing an MBA in record time, he was invited to join the training programme at Goldman, but a chance meeting with Goal One's founder had changed all that.

Paul briefly explained what had come up and asked his brother if he could stay over, at least for that night, perhaps longer. No problem, his brother answered - he had to go to Europe and the Far East on business that night anyway and he would be gone for a few weeks. He would tell the concierge that Paul would be staying.

Paul sat back in the cab. As an afterthought, he turned his head to look through the back window of the cab. It was only after he had done this a few times that he noticed a vehicle which seemed to be going the same way; it must be following him.

It was a dark blue Lexus.

The Lexus stayed behind the cab until they reached his brother's address. Only then did it pass.

Paul paid the driver, got out and scanned the street. The Lexus seemed to have vanished. If he had been a little more observant, he would have noticed the black Cherokee which was passing at that very moment.

Before Paul went inside the building, he dialled one more number – Carolina's.

'Hello?'

'Carolina – it's Paul in New York.'

'Well, well Mr Lawyer, what can I do for you? There was laughter in her voice.

'I was thinking of going away for a few days, so it's either the Hamptons or some clubbing in Miami' he said, still on the lookout for the dark blue Lexus. 'The Hamptons is not really a place for a young, handsome NY lawyer to wind down, and Miami.....'

'....has plenty of wealthy old women at any time of the year!' Carolina continued, again with a laugh.

'I hadn't thought of that one, but now you mention it...' countered Paul.

'So what are your plans then, really? I'm supposed to be going to São Paulo on business but I haven't made any arrangements. Yet.'

'No problem – I'll call you when I'm in town and we'll see' said Paul, trying to sound as if he didn't care either way.

Carolina laughed softly. 'Come on Mr Lawyer – that's the best you can do to convince me? Not very impressive!'

Paul had a flash of inspiration.

'OK – a moonlight boat trip with dinner for two on Elliott Key?'

Elliott Key was one of the most beautiful spots around Miami, only reachable by boat, and now part of the Biscayne National Park.

'Now we're getting somewhere!' said Carolina. 'Call me when you've reached town and we'll discuss it further. Got to run!' and she rang off.

At that moment the Lexus drove by. Anfield turned quickly and disappeared inside the building. He packed again in his brother's apartment, and was quickly on his way again. He gave the doorman a healthy tip and went out through a back alley. There he caught another cab.

His plan was to go to La Guardia and fly American to Miami. During the cab ride he checked several times for the Lexus, but it was not there.

A few minutes into the ride, Carolina called him back. Her brother was just finishing some business near Jersey and was on his way back to Teterboro, the foremost New York airport for private planes. Would Paul like to fly down to Miami with her brother?

Paul gladly accepted. He got the details of the plane and she said she would call her brother to inform him of the extra passenger.

The plane was a Falcon Citation, painted dark red with large letters saying 'Monterey Industrias' and the company's logo. It touched down at Kendall-Tamiami somewhere around one in the morning. Kendall-Tamiami is one of Florida's busiest private airports, and although Paul had landed there several times on business, he was always amazed how busy it was, even after midnight.

As he came down the steps from the jet behind Carolina's brother Jorge, the Florida heat and humidity enveloped Paul like a blanket. The smell of the Miami night air, the kerosene and jet fumes combined with the sound of departing, landing or taxing jets. The scene made a unique panorama, with the lightning surrounding the airstrip.

An Audi A8 and a Chevrolet Blazer, both black, were standing close to the steps, surrounded by people. Both cars were on Mexican DF plates.

Jorge didn't talk much with Paul on the flight from New York. He was one of her older brothers and was clearly in charge of a substantial part of the family business. He was polite, but non-committal. When one of the team in the two cars spoke to him, he turned around and offered Paul a ride to his hotel. Paul accepted.

The two of them settled in the back of the Audi, which had both tinted windows and bullet proof glass, Paul noticed. Jorge had seen Paul touching the car's window and explained that the vehicle was normally used by their father when he was in Mexico, but it had been brought to Miami to confuse any possible abduction intentions.

Jorge hit his two cellphones the moment they had settled, and the Audi left for the airport exit while the Chevrolet on its tail turned on to the Dolphin Expressway. The drivers of the two cars clearly had little patience with the 55 mph speed limits and were soon passing the rest of the traffic. Jorge spoke continuously in Spanish on the two phones, making notes on some papers during the flight.

Less than 20 minutes after leaving the airstrip, Paul had been dropped at the entrance of his hotel, the Montevideo Towers, close to South Pointe. He had been able to call ahead from New York to one of the hotel's owners, who was a client of Paul's firm. The Monte, as it was usually called, was one of Miami's most famous boutique hotels. It had been designed on a large scale yet still remained cosy and intimate.

The two cars arrived at speed, the security team leaving them almost before the cars had stopped moving. Less than a minute later, they were gone again.

Paul checked into the hotel, mentioned his reservation and got a suite at a reasonable price. He headed for the elevators.

In the meantime back in New York, both the teams who had been following him had realised he had given them the slip.

Not for long. The moment he used his credit card at the hotel, their computer systems told them exactly where he was.

La Unidad was the first to scramble a unit to follow him. While Paul was still asleep in his room, a Chevrolet Blazer rolled up and parked close to the hotel entrance. Inside it, a woman made a call on a secure cellphone.

'Ya, lo hemos comprobado, el tipo esta en la habitacion 125 que es un suite y bastante lejos de los ascensores' she said. His room is well away from the lifts.

The man sitting beside her sat back. La Unidad had arrived.

The next day Paul called Carolina and told her he would pick her up around five o'clock to take her to Elliott Key. They arranged to meet at the entrance of the Hilton Fontainebleau.

Paul spend the rest of the day working on the Kaneko files. Then he organised a rental car and called an old friend, a man called Johnny Lorimar, whom he knew from his military service days. Johnny was in the boating business, especially powerboats, just like his father before him. He said he could lend Paul a Cigarette. Johnny and the Lorimar family business looked after the boats used by Florida's coastguard, so the quality of his service was guaranteed.

Paul arranged to pass by after lunch at his Thunder Alley offices near Sunny Isles Beach, so they could talk before he took the boat out. It was all within a 30-minute drive of Collins Avenue, so it would be easy to pick up Carolina.

Paul left his hotel after lunch in a rented Hertz open Mustang and headed for Thunder Alley along the Biscayne Boulevard. The weather was typical of Miami – blue skies, light breeze and comfortable humidity for the time of the year.

His Mustang was followed discreetly by the Blazer, now with a fresh team driving it. It was the Blazer driver who noticed that somebody else was also following the Mustang. He watched for a few moments to make sure, then called for instructions.

The orders came back crisp and clear – just stay with the lawyer and his car, don't engage in anything.

The other car following was a Ford Crown Victoria. So far the people inside it hadn't noticed that the Chevrolet was also tailing Paul. Only when Paul left Biscayne Boulevard and took the turning for Maule Lake on 826, the Sunny Isles Boulevard, did the occupants of the Ford realise another car was sharing the chase. They too reported their observation, supplied the licence number of the Blazer and receiving the same instructions – stay with the lawyer, don't engage.

It was through the licence plates that John Cushing knew an hour later that Paul Anfield had become of interest to others. The plates were registered to a Miami-based company which was under the investigation of the DEA. The company was suspected to be part of a money recycling infrastructure, and was related to some Mexican gangs from the Sinaloa cartel.

Paul stayed at Johnny's office for some 45 minutes before walking towards a jetty where a number of powerboats lay moored. The two men climbed aboard a light blue Cigarette Café Racer. Having shown him the boat, Johnny climbed back onshore to cast it off. Its impressive engines fired up, and slowly the Cigarette left the harbour.

The occupants of both cars called in, and both received the same instructions, to stay put. Paul in the meantime had turned the Cigarette towards the direction of Miami Beach centre and continued for about 30 minutes parallel with Collins Avenue. When he saw the majestic Fontainebleau arise on his left, he found a place to tie up.

The sound of the Cigarette's engines had attracted some onlookers from other boats moored. A deckhand from another boat helped him fasten the Cigarette and Paul cut the engines. Paul gave the deckhand some dollars and asked him if he would keep an eye on it while he was gone. Then he crossed Collins Avenue and walked towards the hotel's entrance.

At that moment, a radiant Carolina appeared. She looked as if she had come from shooting a commercial in the Miami sun. She wore tight figure-hugging light blue pants, a dark blue shirt emblazoned with a Gulf Oil logo and a smile which stopped Paul dead in his tracks.

She took the initiative, running into his arms and kissing him on both cheeks. A woman shouldn't smell so good, thought Paul as their bodies parted again.

'Well Mr Lawyer – welcome to Miami!' she smiled, still not letting go of Paul.

'The pleasure is mine! Come on!' and he took her by the hand. People entering and leaving looked with healthy envy at this male and female eye candy amidst a typical riffraff of tourists and elderly people in loud clothes.

They crossed the hotel drop-off and parking area, waited for the traffic lights to change and crossed Collins again to reach the Cigarette, talking all the time. Paul thanked the sailor who had been watching the boat and helped him to untie her, while Carolina stepped in, clearly used to this sort of thing.

The motor launch's two mighty Mercury engines kicked into life and they slowly gathered speed, heading for the bridges of Julia Tuttle and

MacArthur Causeway. Carolina looked with frowning eyes, wondering where he was taking them. Paul smiled and shrugged his shoulders. The raw, booming sound of the twin engines made any conversation impossible, particularly when they headed out into Biscayne Bay and Paul opened the throttle.

Some 20 minutes later they passed the Boca Chita Lighthouse on their left. The late afternoon sun was casting a unique glow over the bay and everything surrounding it.

Paul cut the engines and they drifted into a little bay with a patch of pale white sand. He went forward and dropped the anchor. Then he returned to the back of the boat, kicked off his docksiders and dropped his pants, revealing a pair of Kiwi French bathing trunks which he had borrowed from his brother's apartment before leaving New York.

On the dashboard of the boat he flicked on the external lights. Then he carried up a large hamper of food he had picked up earlier that day through the concierge of the hotel, along with a large blanket.

Carolina looked at him with a smile, saying nothing. Then she also undid her pants.

'Pity, I thought I was going to catch you out' he said, admiring her tanned legs.

'Sorry Mr Lawyer, but I'm used to the Keys' Carolina answered. She followed Paul over the side of the boat into the shallow, warm water. They started to wade towards the little patch of white sand.

Paul prepared the towel and started unpacking the hamper. Then he went in search of some dead branches to make a small fire.

They settled on the big beach blanket and began to enjoy the silence and watch the sea. The fire relieved some of the approaching darkness, and the full moon did its best to help.

Paul started to talk. He told Carolina everything - where he came from, where he had studied, his professional life, the influence of his uncle, his family. Everything except Kaneko. He paused only to fill up their glasses with white wine from one of the chilled bottles he had brought along.

When he stopped, it was Carolina's turn. They went on talking for hours, stopping only to have some food.

The Keys night was dark and warm and the chemistry between them was like a storm building. Suddenly Carolina got up in the middle of a sentence and started to undo her shirt. She dropped it on the sand, shook her hair and held out her hand. 'Come on' she said.

Paul took in the spectacular sight of Carolina's body, covered only by a tiny red bikini. The light of the fire seemed to melt into her golden skin. Her dark hair and trained, tanned body reminded him of the impression he had had of her on the day of his uncle's funeral. He was reminded of Raquel Welch in her late twenties. The bikini hugged every curve of her body.

He got up, feeling like a schoolboy. One part of his body had become very aroused. Thank god for Bermuda swimming trunks.

They walked into the water, holding hands. Carolina bent over and seemed to cup some water, but then she dashed it over a startled Paul. She laughed and ran on into the water, lit only by the full moon.

They reached deep water and started swimming. Then they floated side by side on their backs, just looking at the moon. Silence again surrounded them.

They turned towards each other and kissed. They drew back and looked at each other, holding each other, kissing again.

After some minutes, Paul suggested it was time to head back for the beach.

'You're a good kisser Mr. Lawyer' she said, swimming alongside him back towards the beach. They walked towards their blanket and settled down; it was easily warm enough to stay the whole night if they wanted to. There was no sound but the soft whisper of sea on sand and the chirruping of the crickets in the undergrowth.

Paul poked the fire and put some more branches on it and they continued to talk, both of them wrapped in towels, switching between their life stories, their good times, bad times, friendships, favourites, work – anything that came to mind.

Finally Carolina got up, unfastened the top of her bikini and put the dark blue shirt back on. Paul was briefly treated to the magnificent sight of her muscular back, her firm bottom and one full breast. When she sat down again, she stepped between his arms and legs and nestled her back into his body for support.

'So what made you really come here? A leading New York lawyer suddenly taking an unplanned break from his deals?' She draped his arms and his towel further around her.

Paul didn't say anything immediately. Should he tell her about Kaneko, his uncle, the murders that had happened over the last few days, why he had left York? The file had awakened some very dangerous people. He was now a part of it, but should he tell his story to this woman? He knew he was falling in love with her, even though they hardly knew each other.

Carolina slowly turned around in his arms and softly pushed him on to his back in the sand. Then she sat on top of him, her hands on his chest. Her eyes had turned into dark pools, the light of the fire sparkling in them.

Slowly she opened her shirt, which had become wet from her damp hair. She tossed it away and bent forward.

This time, there was no restraint, no control. Just instinct and passion. They seemed immediately to find the rhythm only very trusted lovers reach over a long period of time.

She stood up, hooked her thumbs into the sides of her bikini bottom and pulled it down. At last she stood in all her beauty above him, while his eyes locked on to her perfect little black bush and the swollen outer lips of her vulva. She was thoroughly aroused. Paul raised himself and placed his hands on her buttocks, his face a few centimeters from her womanhood.

He waited a second before burying his face and tongue inside her. It was only a few moments before she let out a healthy shout of relief.

Paul tried to continue, but she pushed his face away.

'Stop….. dejame' she said, pushing him gently back against the towel. In a swift move, she helped him out of his Bermudas, knelt and surveyed his fully erect cock.

'You were first in line when God was handing out ze extras' she said in a deep husky voice, imitating a Mexican accent.

'And how would you know, señorita?' Paul murmured, in a voice strained by physical impatience.

She grabbed him, moving her hair to one side so Paul could have an undisturbed view of his cock moving in and out of her mouth, while her tongue played around his glans. She drew her mouth away just long enough to answer him briefly.

'A combination, señor, of a big family, lots of older brothers, mucho boyfriends…'

Paul was nearly bursting. He released himself from her grip and sat up, while she slid her body under him. She opened her legs and guided him inside her in one swift, fluid movement.

Their lips locked in a kiss and his shaft entered her like a piston, his balls hitting her swollen vulva.

CHAPTER 23

It was all over very quickly. But both the lovers knew that soon, very soon, more would follow.

They both came with the raw power of pent-up strength and lust. Then slowly they relaxed.

'Wow!' said Paul

'Wow' Carolina answered.

There were a few moment of closeness together on the warm sand, then they helped each other to their feet, kissed and ran laughing out into the sea again.

In the hours that followed, Paul finally spilt the beans. He told Carolina everything. Yet even as he did so he felt a nagging fear that he had made her part of a potentially highly dangerous situation, one whose end could not yet be foreseen.

They talked through the night, analysing the situation, considering what could be done.

Again they made love and again they swam. Finally they curled up together on the beach blanket and slept.

It was the sun that woke them, a golden early-morning Florida sun already warming the sand. They decided to head for Miami and breakfast. All the way back in the Cigarette, Carolina did not let go of Paul.

The site of the speeding launch, its engines at full throttle, and the golden couple on board was caught only by a few fishermen and early boaters. They again attracted attention when the Cigarette moored at Thunder Alley. Paul introduced Carolina and they thanked Johnny for the use of the boat. They grabbed their belongings and the bag with towels and the remains of their dinner. Then they were heading back to Paul's hotel in the rented Mustang.

The Blazer and the Ford Crown again followed, each manned by new teams. A woman had joined the lawyer, the reports said. A very beautiful one.

Do not engage, the order came back.

Paul and Carolina drove back over Collins Avenue and decided to stop for a moment at the family compound on Indian Creek for Carolina to pick up some fresh clothes. During their drive, she had been looking in the side mirror of the Mustang. As a girl growing up with security always surrounding her and her family, she was accustomed to being always on the alert. Long before they reached the right turn from Collins into the Indian Creek Island road which would lead to the 91st Street security barrier – the only entrance into Indian Creek – she had spotted both the Blazer and the Ford Crown.

She took out her mobile, dialled a number and spoke briefly in rapid Spanish. When they reached the Indian Creek Island road, she told Paul to turn round and park in front of a large deli shop called Cantina Cubana.

'You've got money?' Paul asked as he parked the Mustang.

'Don't worry – just wait in the car, I'll be back in ten'. She gave him a long kiss, got out of the car and crossed to the shop.

She was greeted warmly by the owner's mother, a Cuban woman with great style. She knew the owners very well. Since her parents had bought the house on Indian Creek more than 25 years before, she and her family had often come here to pick up food at any time of the day or night.

'Carolina, estas radiante! How are your parents? What can I do for you?'

'Gracias, all very well. Angelica, did Pepe or Ramon come to the shop?

'Yes yes – go to the back. They have both just come.'

Carolina knew her way around the shop as if it was her own. In the back there was a special area where a small window served hot and cold food to a select number of workers, all of them involved in the security and well-being of the residents of Indian Creek. About five long tables were always set and they were usually occupied, often by police officers.

She found the two men she had called already waiting for her. Ramon was the head of her father's security detail and Pepe took care of her mother. Both were Mexican, ex DEA and Special Forces, and both had been with her family for a long time.

Carolina came straight to the point. Somewhere near the front there were two cars which had been tailing her. She gave the descriptions and asked the men to see what they could find out. Both men hurried away, speaking into small walkie-talkies. Carolina knew that with the contacts these men had in law enforcement in Florida and further afield, she would very soon know something.

She went back through the front of the store, hugged Mrs Angelica again and returned to the parked Mustang. Then they continued into 91st Street and entered the security barrier of the compound.

Nobody followed, or could follow. Indian Creek is only open to residents or people invited by residents, and only with prior clearance. She told Paul how to get to her father's house.

As they entered a long driveway which was guarded at its entrance, she explained that two brothers and an uncle had all built houses relatively close to each other - a kind of a compound within a compound.

They parked in front of the largest house, which closely resembled a

Mexican hacienda. Waiting for them were two maids, who welcomed Carolina with reverence but great warmth.

A large white golden retriever came running at Carolina, wagging its tail like a white flag.

'You coming in, or you prefer to wait? There is nobody at home, so don't worry about being inspected!' she said with a laugh.

'I'll wait. What's the dog's name?'

'Rudy.' She went up the stairs to the entrance and disappeared into the house.

Paul walked with the dog over the beautifully-kept lawn towards the waterfront, which gave a clear view towards Biscayne Point and beyond. To his left was a small boat house, and some technicians were busy with the engine compartment of a cherry red Donzi. Beside it another man was polishing a beautiful Riva Aquarama.

Paul walked on and took a quick look at the other Monterey houses, all with one type of boat or another in front. Rudy was still dutifully following him.

When he turned, he saw Carolina walking towards him. She had put on some jeans and some white Todds and a white cotton shirt. As they walked back to his car, she told him some of the history of the houses and the people living in them.

One of the maids put a small leather bag in the back of the car with some fresh clothes. Then they drove back towards Miami and Paul's hotel for breakfast.

As they were going down Collins Avenue, Carolina's phone rang. She listened, closed the phone and she put it back in her pocket. Then she looked in the side mirror.

'We are being followed by two cars' she said. 'One belongs to a defence foundation in Maryland and the other to a company possibly related to the Sinaloa cartel. We have special babysitters, that's for sure. I would like to meet more of your friends!' she laughed.

Paul didn't say anything. He was concentrating on the traffic while trying to spot in his mirrors which cars were trailing them. He was not surprised by Carolina's coolness. As the daughter of a wealthy Mexican businessman, she would be well used to personal security.

At the Monte they went up to his suite, stopping at the concierge's desk to order a large breakfast. Carolina went straight out on to the terrace and looked over the water towards Fisher Island. Paul had dropped their stuff on a chair and followed her on to the terrace.

He stood behind her and held her tight.

'I'm sorry, but I had to tell you about the situation, this Kaneko file and what's been happening. But you can't stay. You should stay with your family and be protected. I can't protect you - I don't know even where to start.'

Carolina turned and looked him in the eye.

'Thank you Paul' she said. 'But I'm afraid I'm in.'

Paul started to say something but she put a finger on his mouth.

'No, wait. I am not a woman who sleeps around, Mr. Lawyer and I'm not sure I like it when my feelings start to rock and roll. You're guilty there. But for the rest I am still somebody who takes her own decisions. So let's be practical – breakfast, shower and a strategy meeting? OK?'

'Oh yes...' she kissed him softly while squeezing him into a full blown erection. 'And please tell your dick it's not always fun time, but I'm glad to know he's a free spirit!' upon which she ran from his arms.

'I'll shower, you wait for breakfast' she said over her shoulder.

He watched her throwing her clothes off. Carolina Monterey had well and truly swept Paul off his feet. It was the first time in his life something like this had happened. Women had come and gone in his life, but this one was totally different. Paul settled on the sofa and switched on the TV set to catch some news and flip through the business channels. Some 20 minutes later, breakfast was delivered.

Carolina appeared from the bathroom in a white hotel bathrobe. Her hair was wet again. He decided that it made her look even more beautiful.

She sat down cross-legged on the bed and watched the news. Paul couldn't help noticing that the way the bathrobe had opened was allowing him to look straight at her beautiful pink womanhood.

'No!' she said when she saw his eyes. 'To the shower, you dirty little lawyer!' But then, instead of rearranging the bathrobe, she opened it a bit further.

Paul got up and started throwing his own clothes around the room, imitating her undressing dance.

'Dios!' she said laughing out loud. 'How silly men look dancing with a hard on!'

Paul showered, put a towel around his waist and came back to finish breakfast. When it was done he went behind the desk in the room and switched on his laptop. He gave Carolina the handwritten notes which he had made over the last few days, plus the copies of the original Kaneko file which he had made before leaving New York.

Morning turned into afternoon. Around two o'clock he looked up from his laptop, feeling hungry. Carolina had been reading all this time, only asking occasional questions and making notes on the hotel stationery.

'Care for lunch?'

She looked up from her papers, which were now spread over the bed.

She said nothing, but put the papers to one side and sat upright on the bed, holding her hand towards him.

He walked to the bed. Before he had reached it, she had opened the bathrobe. The sun was shining into the room and her beauty merged into the light, just like last night on the beach.

Gently he took her in his arms and carried her naked to the couch. His towel had fallen away and his erection was brushing her body.

For the next 30 minutes, no words were spoken which were longer than one syllable.

Finally they showered again, tidied the room and the papers, and headed downstairs for lunch by the hotel pool.

Outside the hotel, one of the men on guard duty inside the Chevrolet Blazer suddenly became alert as two black Cherokees pulled up in front of the entrance. All four doors of each car opened in unison. A tall and very elegant elderly man had got out of the lead Cherokee, and seemed to be clearly in charge. He spoke to the rest of his group, turned and entered the hotel lobby, followed by one of his men.

'Federales' said one of the men in the Blazer.

'O similar. Mejor llamas al central' said the other. Better call Control.

But even as he spoke, three men from the second Cherokee started walking towards their car. When they reached the Blazer, two hung back while the first man tapped the driver's window. He showed his DSA ID.

'DSA' he said. 'Please be so kind as to remove your car.'

The Colombian driver was a hardened but very disciplined ex-Colombian Special Forces Captain but who had joined La Unidad years earlier for purely financial reasons. He knew his orders – no engagement, specially with people like the DSA.

He held the DSA man's gaze for a moment. These must be the men from the Ford Crown which they had spotted the previous day following the lawyer.

He started the Chevrolet's engine, closed the window and drove off.

CHAPTER TWENTY THREE

In his rear-view mirror he could see the men returning to their Cherokee.

So they'd called in the DSA.

Less than two minutes later, Felipe Lisker received a very brief call from an untraceable number. The message received meant that he was going to have to speak with someone he hadn't had contact with for a very long time. Marcus Wellington had founded the DSA, and used its resources during their joint business venture.

It meant that the information assembled by his old lawyer Gerstner was moving in the one direction it shouldn't – into the open.

Lisker excused himself from the dinner he had organised at his favourite private members' club, the Fox, off London's Piccadilly. He went up the stairs to his suite, closed the door carefully behind him and sat behind the large mahogany table. On a secured file within his PC, which had been prepared by La Unidad and therefore was practically impossible to crack, he found a name, a telephone number and a fax number. He rang the number, identified himself and waited for confirmation. The voice came back with an email address. Then the connection was broken.

Lisker emailed a single line of text to address. It read 'Kaneko 0052176865790'. The number was a special telephone line which would re-direct the caller to Lisker's UK cellular number without leaving any trace.

Now he had to wait for the call. From whom he didn't know, but certainly someone with executive powers.

He sat back, put his feet up on the writing desk and re-lit his cigar. He was going to do everything to solve this matter and take care that the Kaneko information disappeared once and for all.

There would be other problems, such was life. With that in mind he picked up the FT which he hadn't had time to read that morning. His guests downstairs could wait. This came first.

CHAPTER 24

In the meantime, a tall, elderly gentlemen who had emerged from one of the DSA Cherokees had crossed the hotel lobby, passed the pool area and entered the restaurant. He soon spotted the people he was looking for and crossed towards them. Heads turned to look at him. A man in a made-to-measure dark suit, shirt and tie in a restaurant beside a pool in the heat of Miami Beach was bound to generate some stares from the idle.

The maître d'hôte tried to follow him, but he was quickly stopped by another man who was discreetly following the first. His DSA badge was enough to keep the man at bay.

The couple were sitting at a table which had a privileged view of the water and the boats passing Fisher Island to go out to sea. They had their backs to him, were holding hands and studying the menu.

'Hello Mr. Anfield.'

Paul looked up.

'And you are?'

'We spoke by phone regarding your uncle.'

'Ah! Mr Wellington. You have come all this way to visit me - though I thought I told you our conversation would not be going any further?'

'Do you mind if I sit down, Mr Anfield?' Wellington did not wait for Paul's agreement before sitting.

'Carolina, meet Marcus Wellington. Mr Wellington - Miss Monterey.'

Wellington got up again briefly to shake Carolina's hand.

A waiter had come to the table. Paul offered Wellington a glass of white wine.

'I see you have got the taste for good wines from your uncle'

196

Wellington said, savouring the perfectly-chilled Crichton Hall chardonnay which Paul had ordered for him and Carolina.

'Mr Wellington, was our phone conversation not clear enough for you?' asked Paul. He was not prepared to engage in conversation a man whom he knew wanted only to stop any leakage of the Kaneko affair.

'You have been very clear. Now let me be equally clear. The Kaneko file is classified material, as from 48 hours ago. Your firm and its partners have been informed accordingly.'

Wellington pulled a letter from his pocket and handed it to Paul. It was on US State Department paper, addressed to Paul. It contained a variety of legal threats concerning what would happen to Paul if he did not comply with its instructions.

'Mr Anfield, I would strongly urge you to hand over all the material you hold on the Kaneko case, either directly or to sources related to you. The US Government is requesting your immediate corporation in the matter. We have given your details to Clayborn Ackerman, who have also been in contact with your firm in New York, as they are the appointed representatives by the US State in this situation.

'Good day. And to you, Miss Monterey.'

Wellington rose from the table and walked away.

Paul and Carolina looked at each other. The US Government was now actively putting its weight behind an orchestrated effort to contain any leakage of the file compiled by Lenny Gerstner.

When Marcus Wellington and his people drove away from the hotel after talking to Paul, Felipe Lisker's phone went off in London. He listened to the message that was being relayed to him – the Federales had now actively joined the chase and made contact directly with a man called Paul Anfield in Miami. Action had to be taken now, or the Federales would be in possession of the Kaneko information.

Lisker told them that he would call back in five minutes with his orders. He got up and walked towards the window and looked out over the pedestrians and cars moving through St James' on a sunny day in London.

Lisker knew one thing – if the Federales, whoever they were, were now the only ones with the files in their possession, this made him the weak link. He could be blackmailed or even taken out by his ex partners. His position had changed completely.

Logic also dictated that the Federales who had been in the game and had now shown themselves also wouldn't want any publicity, of any kind.

He took a decision, went back to the desk and speed-dialled a number on his phone.

'Conectame con Chepa en Miami.'

Chepa was on the other end within seconds.

'Cuanta gente tienes disponible cerca del hotel?' How many men are available?

'Un coche.'

'Tell them to follow the Federales and organise an interception. No survivors y sin testigos…' No witnesses.

Silence.

'Patron, son Federales!' Chepa came back.

'We have the surprise element on our side – they will not expect an attack. Have they left the hotel?'

'Un momento…'

Click.

Chepa came back on: 'They're leaving the hotel right now.'

'OK – call me with the results.' Lisker rang off.

Chepa was sitting somewhere near Palmetto Expressway in an office building which was doubling as a communications hub for La Unidad. He was already dialling from a different phone to give instructions to the unit to follow the DSA Cherokees.

Disciplined as he was as a military man, Chepa always had one or more back-up units in the area, which he now contacted. His instructions were clear to all his people - take out all the passengers in both cars. The Unidad units made contact and plotted the best place to intercept the vehicles. Given the direction the Cherokees were heading, they guessed they were going towards Miami International, the nearest airport. That meant the only place to stage an attack which provided adequate escape routes was the Dolphin Expressway. The second La Unidad unit headed towards the entrance of 27th Avenue.

In the meantime in the DSA Cherokee, Marcus Wellington was thinking about Paul Anfield and wondering what the lawyer would do next. Would he do the sensible thing and hand over his Kaneko files, or would he continue to make trouble? Hostile action could come only in one form – exposing the information in the press. He stared out of the window. They were now entering the expressway leading towards the airport.

The two La Unidad vehicles tailed the DSA men from 27th Avenue onwards. The second of these was a souped-up Bronco with a handheld Soviet build RPG-7 grenade launcher on board, now in the confident grip of an ex-Peruvian paratrooper. Traffic was relatively light on Dolphin for the time of day. They decided to launch the attack at the level of NW 31st Street.

The Bronco slowly pulled alongside the second Cherokee, while the other La Unidad unit, in the Chevrolet Blazer which had been in front of the hotel, was slightly in front of the Cherokee carrying Marcus Wellington.

Given that no special alert or threat had been flagged when the DSA units had been informed that morning of Wellington's visit, the four agents had no reason to expect trouble. In any case they were armed only with standard handguns.

The ex-paratrooper fired the RPG-7 just as the driver of the lead DSA car spotted the two La Unidad vehicles. The rocket's impact practically blew the second Cherokee over the safety barrier of the expressway.

The Blazer was now alongside the lead Cherokee. A single shot through the window killed the driver before he had any idea what was happening. The agent in the back seat behind him fell to a second shot. Now the Blazer wedged the driverless Cherokee against the security barrier to slow it down.

Marcus Wellington stared in disbelief at the wreckage of the second DSA car, which had now practically come to a stop on the hard shoulder. Only then did he realised that he had been sprayed with something wet and sticky - the blood and brain tissue of his driver.

He looked at the man slumped sideways on the back seat. The window on the other side shattered. The Blazer had now wedged the car hard into the safety barrier, and a rain of metal sparks flew up from the metal-to-metal contact.

The two cars had stopped, the Bronco a few meters in front. The rest of the traffic was swerving towards the centre of the expressway to avoid them.

Before the cars had come to a complete halt, the man in the front passenger seat of the Blazer had thrown down his Colt 45 and grabbed an Uzi. He now used it to spray Marcus Wellington with its full 600-rounds-per minute firepower. The impact of the 9mm Parabellum bullets tore into Wellington's body. For a moment he seemed to dance in his seat.

The Blazer pulled away. No smoking tyres; he simply drove off as if nothing had happened. These were professionals.

Nobody stopped. Traffic continued to swerve around the wreckage of the two Cherokees.

From the Bronco, the ex Peruvian paratrooper leaned out, took aim at Wellington's Cherokee with the RPG-7 grenade launcher and discharged another grenade. The car exploded. By the time the first motorists began to stop to see what was going on, both the Blazer and the Bronco were nearly at the exit of 14th Street.

It was another 15 minutes before the Metro Dade County police appeared on the scene.

CHAPTER 25

Back at the hotel, Paul and Carolina had gone back to their room after Wellington had left. They gave the documents another going over.

'What are you going to do with it all?' asked Carolina. Are you going to hand over all this information?'

Paul said nothing, but went over to the desk where they had gathered the rest of the papers before lunch.

'I've got to think.'

'You mean we've got to think. You're not in this alone, you know.' She stepped up behind him and wrapped her arms around his body.

'I'm sorry I got you into this.'

'I've always liked hanging out with the wrong kinds of guys, according to my mother.' She gently kissed him. 'Let's see where we are.'

'Here is how I see it' Paul began. 'The people who started all this divide into two factions. There's the US Government, backed by the technical help of Lenny Gerstner and coordination by Marcus Wellington and others. On the other we have a strategically-placed Colombian coffee grower called Lisker providing the land on the Colombian, Brazilian and Peruvian border to accommodate military actions. The US Government starts using the Lisker facility.' The pair of them sat down on the couch.

'Lisker was probably already involved in the drugs trade, but the opportunity to use US Government planes and US Army facilities on US soil was too good to miss.'

He started to massage Carolina's breasts, but she pushed his hands away.

'Concentrate, Mr Lawyer!'

Paul smiled. 'It enabled him to become the owner of a drugs air bridge between Colombia and its biggest market – the USA. Then, some years later, Lisker decides he wants to leave the business. At first Uncle Lenny has been an unwitting facilitator in setting up all the operating structures, tax vehicles, trusts or whatever to push the money back into the system. Now he begins to understand that Lisker hasn't been making all this money in the coffee trade.

'Then Lisker gets lucky: US administrations start changing their political tack on South America, the war on drugs escalates, and he has made more money under the coverage of the US Government than he could ever have imagined. So he closes down and moves his business out of the Lewman setting. Now my uncle can get out of the front line.'

Paul had started massaging Carolina's lower back and was now slipping his hands into her jeans.

'My uncle, however, wants to clear the decks before his time comes. So he starts putting a file on Kaneko together. Technically speaking that's easy – he's handled the Lisker and Mercado Libre accounts over the years on his own.

'When his secretary died in that plane crash, the information was concentrated even more on him.

'Then he dies, and the file appears on the desk of the Lewman managing partner, who tells me - because I'm family.'

'Stop!' gasped Carolina. 'I'm getting wet. I won't have enough underwear left if you go on like this! Concentrate!' She pulled his hands out of her jeans.

Paul laughed and rolled on to the floor, then got up to fetch some mineral water. He handed her a bottle.

'Suddenly Lisker and the US Government, through Wellington, are faced with the resurfacing of information which should never have existed in the first place. Wellington knows it would cover the whole of Washington – not just himself – in the proverbial shit. The US Government partnering a drugs dealer for all those years?

'Lisker in the meantime has become a respectable, but always discreet, international businessman. He's recycled himself. So he doesn't want that either.'

Carolina had suddenly got up from the couch and walked over to the TV, which was on but with the sound turned off. Marcus Wellington's face had appeared on the screen.

As she switched on the sound, the picture changed to a scene on an expressway, apparently of some major accident. There were police cars and fire trucks, and at least two cars appeared to be on fire.

'Both vehicles appear to have been struck by a number of shots' the reporter was saying. 'We're told that at least five people have died and we do know that one of these men has been identified as Senator Marcus Wellington, the Chairman of the International Security Board. No witnesses has yet come forward.'

Paul and Carolina looked at each other.

'We've got to go' said Paul. 'Now.' His voice was numb with shock

Carolina did not argue. Within a few minutes they had packed up their belongings and were checking out of the hotel. Paul gave the concierge a hefty tip and asked if a cab could pick them up at the service entrance of the hotel. He also gave him the keys to the rental car and asked him to call Hertz to pick it up.

As they waited for the cab to show up, they discussed where to head for. After throwing around a number of alternatives, they settled on hiding in plain sight – Cozumel, Mexico. Carolina knew it through a friend of hers in the tourist rental business who had some houses on the quiet part of the island.

Not knowing if their cellphones were being intercepted, she used the switchboard of the hotel to reach her friend. They were lucky – she had a phone available. Carolina told her to send the bill to her house.

After hanging up, she had a suggestion for Paul: why not ask her relatives if she could use the family plane to drop them off in Cozumel? She didn't wait for Paul's agreement to make the call.

They were lucky. The plane had to go to Mexico to pick up her father and some friends the next day, but Carolina's brother said it was no problem if the plane went that night.

Ten minutes later they were heading for Kendall-Tamiami airport, where the Monterey jet was waiting fuelled and ready to go.

They were able to sleep briefly during the flight to Cozumel. On arrival they thanked the pilot and flight attendant and were waved through by the single customs official. They boarded a cab and Carolina gave the driver the address of the house, which was between Throne and El Mirador.

They would have succeeded in leaving the USA without being spotted if La Unidad had not already asked its people to be on the lookout for Paul, and circulated a photograph. La Unidad usually had friends in public places like airports. It was one of the crew servicing the Monterey jet who overheard the reason for the change of flight plan - one of the Monterey daughters needed to be dropped off on Cozumel island before the flight continued to Mexico DF tomorrow. That same crew member also overheard them say a man would be joining the flight.

He called in, just in case it was important. His La Unidad contact listened, thought for a moment and then said that he would arrange for a photograph of their target to be sent. Before the aircraft took off, a photograph was handed to the man at Kendall-Tamiami, so when the cab dropped Carolina and Paul off an hour and a half later, the man from the refuelling services knew immediately that he had found their man.

While all this was happening, Juan Chepa placed a call to Lisker in London to report the successful killing of Wellington, with no witnesses and no evidence. Lisker excused himself from the corner table of the Claridges Hotel restaurant and went to the foyer.

'Bien hecho. What about the Anfield guy?'

'He must still have the information.'

'The Federales should have taken care of his firm in New York. They're good at looking after that kind of thing, and corporate lawyers don't to go to war with their government. So the Anfield guy is on his own. Even more so now if he sees the news on TV.'

'Patron – he's been with a woman now for the past few days.'

Silence. Lisker was thinking. The odds that the US Government, the Federales would go after him were remote; Wellington's history and all the dirty business were best buried. A fully-fledged manhunt for his killers might draw press interest. The deaths of four DSA agents was just collateral damage. So this left only one part to be settled - the Anfield guy, now apparently accompanied by a woman.

'Terminalo. Los dos, but try to make it look like an accident.' Lisker ended the call.

Chepa and his men would need a few more days of preparation, but that was a manageable risk. If they struck now, the fact that Wellington had been at the same hotel would perhaps trigger further investigations by the Federales. If confirmation came from Chepa that Anfield and the woman with him had been taken care of, then it would look as if the problem had been dealt with.

Lisker went back to his table. After lunch he would start to concentrate on the matter in Spain - the loss of his participation in

BANINSA via the Virtuvio holdings after the intervention by the Banco de España. He had to deal with them, but even more importantly with Emilio de Ronin and his partners, who, as he had already found out through Rheinman, was in the front running for the takeover of BANINSA.

Lisker asked the waiter for a cigar. You had to enjoy every day of your life, he reflected.

CHAPTER 26

When Paul and Carolina arrived at the island on the Aeromexico flight from Mexico City to Cozumel, two passengers had joined the flight after connecting from one which had arrived that morning from Bogotà. According to their passports they were Augusto Lafita and Jorge Mercader, two sailors who were supposed to board a vessel for a private cruise to sail around the Gulf of Mexico. They were to leave Cozumel on a ship via Mezcalito.

The men were dressed like thousands of others who were milling around Mexico DF Airport – jeans, sneakers, white polo shirts. They slipped effortlessly through the crowds, eyes constantly sweeping around but not making eye contact with anybody.

In reality they were brothers, Pablo and Pedro Cochabamba, better known as Los Hermanos and two of the most respected professional assassins available on the Colombian market. They had been trained by their father, a textbook sadist called Jorge who had founded one of the first training centres for scisarios, the name given to the young killers who Pablo Escobar and others from the cartels used from the seventies onwards.

Jorge, who had killed his wife, mother of Pablo and Pedro, during one of his uncontrollable anger attacks, had trained his sons to become the best in their business. But he took care of one thing: they were going to operate as independents. The highest bidder would get their services. No exclusivity for anybody. So after completing their training, they moved away from their hometown of Cali to Bogotà.

Contracts came quickly. First through their father, but as their reputation grew after each successful job, so the work kept coming in.

Los Hermanos gained their reputation by being utterly effective. No contract was unfulfilled.

Even more important was their professional standing. Unlike many hired killers, especially Colombian ones, they did a clean job. They always avoided public killings. Their reasoning was simple; the more professional the job, the less police would try to solve the case. Professional hits left very few traces for the investigators. Such clean work was highly valued.

The brothers each had specific qualities. They took care that one supported the other by using the specific skill needed for each job.

This contract came along the established route - a small ad in one of Bogotà's newspapers, repeated over a number of days, requesting advice on the export of coal to Spain and leaving a cellphone number. The contracting party then waited until a call to the number was placed from a public phone booth, agreeing to a meeting in a public place.

The first arranged meeting was usually to give the brothers the opportunity to have a look at the other party without making contact with them, and check that they were not followed. The prospective client was watched, their immediate environment surveyed. The next day the brothers would call the number again from a different phone booth and agree a new rendezvous, again in a hotel or similar public place.

For their own security reasons, the brothers would let the other party sit and wait for a while. After 10 to 15 minutes, one of them would establish contact by approaching the other party. Meanwhile the other brother stayed near, with a compact automatic weapon at the ready in case it proved to be a set-up. Their father had taught them that you never knew what fallout you might get from an earlier job.

Usually Pedro made the physical contact, leaving Pablo waiting with his favourite silenced Heckler & Koch G36, loaded and with the safety off. Pablo liked using the silencer. If he needed to act, the element of sheer surprise in combination with silent shooting gave him valuable seconds to take out targets near his brother.

A few years before, this had happened in Bogotà's Westin Crown Hotel and the story of the shooting had appeared in the Colombian newspapers. Between them the brothers had killed three people and injured 10 more. Since that time, the brothers had established this as standard routine. No meetings took place separately. Wherever Pablo was, Pedro would be within 50 meters.

This time the contract handlers handed them a pen drive with a description of the targets, their location and photographs. The other information on the drive was just to give additional background. In this case it was a man and a woman, clearly on the run, so time was important.

Instructions were clear. The targets were in hiding about 25 miles south of Cozumel, but they could leave at any moment.

After studying the information on the pen drive, Pablo went to an internet café and sent a pre-agreed email accepting the contract. A few days later they received confirmation from their Bahamian bank that the 75% down payment had been received. In the meantime Pablo had taken care of the logistics, making sure the necessary weapons would be available for them when they arrived in Mexico.

As usual for such contracts, the brothers had a number of contacts who took care of this sort of thing. These men were very highly rewarded runners who for the right price would take care of everything. The brothers had been taught that cutting corners to save money would inevitably cause problems. As in any highly-specialised business, as little as possible should be left to chance or bad luck. Given that they changed passports at least once during such engagements, the forgeries had to be perfect. The same for weapons. You couldn't have a gun jamming or malfunctioning during a hit.

For this contract they had decided to use a .308 hunting rifle with a Zeiss Ikon telescopic site attached and hollow-point ammunition. They also asked for an Israeli TCI M89SR compact sniper rifle to be shipped through their usual channels to Cozumel. It used the same ammunition.

Through the internet they had already studied as far as possible the coastline where the targets where hiding out. The beach was about 100 to 150 metres from the tree line. For either brother to take the shot at that distance was an easy matter. Pedro had once taken out a target at more than 700 meters from a moving car.

Pablo reasoned that if the targets were a man and a woman they were presumably in a relationship. They would be spending time on the beach, and surely would be going for a swim at some point. This would give them the perfect opportunity to make the hit.

Pedro would rent a small fishing boat and wait some miles out of the coast while Pablo made the hit. Once the targets had been taken care of, Pablo would call his brother, either by cellphone or two-way radio, to come inshore and help him take the bodies out to sea. The salt water and the sharks would take care of the clean-up.

The brothers had left Bogotà for a flight to Lima a few days before. A day later they boarded their flight for Mexico, with a through connection to Cozumel. When the brothers arrived at Cozumel Airport, two men were waiting for them; trusted members of the Cartel del Golfo whom the brothers used for organisational issues. They had a long-running arrangement with its capo, Pedro Cocobamba, aka Loco Bomba.

Several connected Gulf Cartel members had used the brothers' services over the years. Every now and then the brothers fulfilled a contract whereby the payment was in kind. They took care of logistics when the Cartel ordered a hit on Mexican soil.

So when Juan Chepa called, Pedro Cocobamba was more than happy to help La Unidad. Many times over the years, La Unidad had been instrumental in helping the cartels. On top of this was of course the very close commercial relationship over drugs transportation into the US market.

During the drive from the airport to the apartment which had been arranged for them in San Miguel, the brothers received additional information on the hit which was going to take place.

'They have hardly left the house' said the cartel man. Pedro was going through a number of photos which clearly had been taken through a telephoto lens from a distance. The photographs showed a man and a woman on the beach, in the surf, sitting on the veranda of a house, shopping at a local market and driving an open buggy.

Neither of the brothers ever gave much attention to the people they had been hired to kill. That was how they'd been trained. Their victims could be fat or slim, tall or short, beautiful or ugly – they didn't care. Distancing themselves from anything remotely human made decisions completely objective. This was their trade, their job. Feelings could only lead to problems.

'Do they get food themselves? Does anyone visit them? What about their communications? Cellphones?' asked Pablo, looking out of the window of the car at nothing specific. He didn't like beach resorts, so he was not interested in the surroundings. Prepare the hit, execute the hit, clean any evidence and get back to Bogotà. That was all that mattered.

'They go to a market nearby. That's it. Since we've been following them, there have been no visits – they keep to themselves. Either the man or the woman has a laptop which they connect with her cellphone.'

The co-driver handed over a detailed map of the El Mirador setting, plus a cross marked in red to show the location of the house.

Traffic was slowing as they reached the coast road where all the major hotels stood. After a few miles the car turned left and headed towards the centre of the island. Five miles later they turned off the road into the driveway of a small house. The car was parked, doors opened and their luggage taken from the trunk. The men entered the house.

Devoid of any real furniture, the living room had a large table and some chairs. They sat down and beer was offered and accepted. One of the men left the room and came back with a lightweight wooden box, which he put on the table.

Pedro opened the box and took out the contents; a weapon which had come through from Mexico DF to the island some days before. He removed the protective wrapping and examined the TCI M89SR, which gleamed with gun oil. He checked it thoroughly and after a few moments put it back in the box.

The man who had brought the weapon left the room and returned with a small box of specially-prepared .308 Winchester plated hollow-point ammunition, as specified. Hollow-point ammunition had a devastating effect – when striking a body the point spread out, destroying far more tissue than a conventional bullet. Autopsy reports of victims killed by such bullets were invariably horror stories.

Once everything had been inspected, the weapons and ammunition were put away. The men finished their beers and decided to head to one of the hotels for food. In the morning they would go with their guides to inspect the killing ground and decide on the final details of the hit.

CHAPTER 27

Paul suddenly woke up some time in the early hours of the following day, still lying on top of the bed. Carolina was sound asleep beside him, naked under the thin white sheet.

He looked at her. Her tanned face had practically turned mahogany, a quick result from their days spend on the beach and walking.

What had woken him? A full erection, the result of a full bladder. Quietly rolling over and taking care not to disturb her, he got out of bed. One thing he had learned about Carolina was that when she slept, she slept. Waking her was quite a task.

Before heading to the bathroom, he took another long look at her. She was the one. The woman he had been waiting for and looking for all his life. He had known as much that day in New York when he had seen her in front of the Four Seasons hotel. These days on the run together had only made his feelings stronger.

When this was over... but he didn't finish his thought. Instead of going back to the bedroom from the bathroom, he walked through the living room out on the veranda.

At four in the morning, the sight of a naked man running into the sea with his member waving freely would have raised eyebrows anywhere.

It was low tide. He ran some distance out into the sea and dived into the waves. Luminous plankton were giving the water a soft green glow. He swam for 10 minutes before wading back to the shore and returning to the house. Then he grabbed a towel and sat on the lower steps of the porch, feet in the sand.

The sun was making its intentions clear, as it did every day at this time. It would soon reign high in a deep blue sky.

Paul got up and looked for his laptop and the connection cable for his cellphone. From his toilet bag he dug out his USB stick. Thank God for law firms and their IT needs.

One of the Lewman clients was a Silicon Valley-based company which had succeeded in manufacturing a USB with a capacity of 8MB, a real feat for those days. The firm was quickly taken over by a VC fund and Paul's firm had to do the legal part of the transaction. At the signing of the sale to the VC, all involved got a semi gold-plated USB stick, engraved with the date of the transaction. Paul had used it wherever he went since the day he had got it.

Now the USB stick held only one kind of file, those related to Kaneko. There were copies of the files his uncle had sent to the firm, plus the notes he had been making since the start, in New York and in Miami and now on Cozumel.

Back on the veranda, he booted the laptop and stuck the USB into one of the slots on the side. The sound of the spinning disc drive echoed the breaking of the waves as the tide began to roll in and the first sounds of birds awakening in the bush behind the house.

When the Sony was ready, Paul read again through some of the files he had saved, corrected a few parts and added some comments. He then connected the Sony to the Nokia and executed a dial-up to his New York office PC, using his secretary's entry codes. Through this connection he was able to enter the partners' back-office administration. The five-year billing history of his uncle for the firm was still there, the names he had already cross-checked back in New York. They were the same names that had been written down in the original Kaneko files.

Paul was more and more convinced that his uncle had known that one day this information would become public. It looked as if he had taken care to see that anybody following the trail had a relatively easy time, as long as they had the file his uncle had prepared and sent to his partners' office shortly before his death.

He felt a hand on his shoulder and looked up to see a naked Carolina. She bent over and kissed him silently.

'You want to see the sun come up?' she asked with a smile. She draped a towel around her and sat down beside him.

'I wanted to send off the email' he said, putting an arm around her. She was silent.

The previous night they had agreed that they had to face a number of realities. They were now free and on the run, but it felt as if the chain of information they had put together was holding them more and more tightly. They knew one thing – nobody was now trying to negotiate with them. The formidable power of the combination of the US Government with its partners in crime simply left them nowhere to go.

The Government had whitewashed its role under the banner of saving democracy at its southern frontiers. The man involved had been killed off – by their partners. After all, a little collateral damage should not be taken out of context. Even less by a commercial lawyer with a highly-reputed Wall Street law firm like Paul, whose own family had been involved in facilitating and structuring the affair.

Against the drug dealers, there was nothing to be done. Their rules were simple - there weren't any.

His uncle should never have felt the remorse which had motivated him to start writing down the whole story. He had signed his death warrant with a blank space instead of a date of completion. Only his untimely natural death had saved him from a more violent one.

Paul knew that the information gathered by his uncle and added to by himself had no value unless and until it could be circulated outside the control of those involved.

He had no contacts in the world of the press, the most obvious direction to turn to. But he did know someone who did.

He started to type.

When he had finished he re-read what he had typed and added the attachments. Then he sent it off. The laptop started slowly purring, confirming that it was following his orders.

'Come on!' called Carolina. She stuck her hand out to him. The towel fell off.

Paul hesitated.

'OK, later' she said.

Paul let out a sigh. 'I can't argue with the bare facts' he said. He put down the computer and got to his feet. Carolina, two steps below him on the sand, pulled his towel away.

With a quick movement she grabbed his already half-erect cock, bent over and took it into her mouth. Paul threw his head back and let out a moan, gently cradling her head in his hands.

But then Carolina let go of his manhood, jumped to her feet and ran laughing towards the sea. He stumbled up and ran after. By the time he had caught her up she was already out in the surf.

They played for some time, swimming, diving and flirting. Finally they walked up from the water and headed, hand in hand, back to the house. They wrapped their towels around them and watched the sun climbing. A breeze had got up, and it was carrying to them the unique smell of the jungle mixed with the sea.

Paul stood behind Carolina and wrapped his arms around her. His hands slipped inside the towel. Softly he started to mould her firm breasts. Her nipples were still hard from their swim.

She started to grind against him. Then she turned around, her hand on his shaft, stroking its full length. They kissed, their towels falling on to the veranda.

Carolina slid one leg around him, opening herself fully and guiding him inside. Paul pulled her up, his shaft firm and warm inside her.

She leaned back.

'You like gymnastics, Mr Anfield?'

'Aaah....'

'I didn't catch that one. That's a yes?' She squeezed her love muscle. Paul laughed loud and pulled her tightly to him.

'Thank you for being you' he said softly, sucking her earlobe.

They continued like this for some time. After a few minutes he filled her again and they climaxed simultaneously. Spent, she laid her head on his shoulder.

'Never leave me' she whispered in his ear, hugging him even closer.

Paul stroked her head softly and hugged her back. 'Time to go to work' he said. He stood up and returned to the laptop.

'I'll make some breakfast' she said, picking up her towel again and giving him a friendly tap on his naked butt.

Paul worked for half an hour, then disconnected the cellphone, took out the USB stick and closed the laptop.

The house had been under surveillance by people with binoculars from the moment Paul and Carolina had arrived. The watchers were taking turns every eight hours. But the man on guard this particular night hadn't seen what Paul was up to with the computer and mobile. He had fallen asleep some time before.

Against orders, he had taken a small bottle of tequila with him. The man was not drunk; he had just reasoned that a little alcohol would help pass the long hours of the night. He had set a silent alarm on his mobile phone for one hour before he was due to go off duty. He was a low-level local cartel soldier, and he didn't know or care why he had been ordered to watch the house. It helped that the girl was so good looking – Paul and Carolina had already given the guards quite a bit of entertainment with their lovemaking sessions on the porch, on the beach and in the sea.

The alarm vibrated about 30 minutes after Paul had packed away his PC and gone inside the house for breakfast. The guard shook himself awake. It was going to be another scorching day. Los grillos were already making their usual incessant racket in the undergrowth.

An hour later, the guard was surprised to see three men coming through the bush towards him. He was expecting only one. And one of the trio was carrying a rifle with a telescopic sight. Not that any of this mattered. His shift was done; he was going home.

He told them there was nothing to report. The couple were inside the house and probably still asleep. He left the same way the three men had come.

Pedro took out the army binoculars which he always took with him on assignments. Now the waiting started. The men made contact periodically with the boat which was cruising some miles offshore.

It was mid-morning when the watchers saw first the man and then the woman appear on the veranda. They looked as if they were going somewhere. They wouldn't be going far; the watchers had made sure of that. The ignition system on the beach buggy they had been using had been cut off.

Pedro started to follow the man through the Zeiss Ikon telescopic sight. First it would be the man, then the woman. First the target, than any expendable witnesses. Another rule their father had taught them.

Through the scope Pablo saw the man leaning against the veranda with a smile on his face. The woman was hurrying back into the house.

'Take it from my wallet!' Paul called after Carolina. She needed cash to do some shopping in the market, one of their favourite pastimes since they had arrived on the island.

Paul turned from the veranda and looked out to sea again. Its beauty and smell could never bore him, particularly knowing that they would have to leave very soon. They might head for Europe; Spain, perhaps.

A sudden silence seemed to descend. All Paul could hear was the sea; no birds, nothing else at all. It was as if nature was on hold.

Even the crickets had stopped their incessant chirruping.

Slowly the normal sounds of a sub-tropical morning returned. Paul shrugged off the moment and headed for the buggy.

'Come on!'

'Coming!' called Carolina. She jumped from the veranda and broke into a short run to catch up with Paul, now astride the buggy.

'Si' said Pablo Cochabamba.

Pedro gently squeezed the trigger of the TCI. The sound of the shot was hard to hear against the surf.

Something gave Paul a mighty kick in the back. He flew forward, his hands outstretched. He wanted to say something, he wanted to get back up again, he wanted... why was the front of his T shirt suddenly wet?

He fell to his knees. His brain shut off, his body collapsed against the buggy. The bullet had destroyed a large part of his heart. Not that there would ever be an autopsy.

Carolina was ten meters behind Paul when she saw him fly forward into the buggy. She watched him try to get to his knees but fall back. He stayed down. He wasn't moving. What was he doing? She started to run towards him.

Then came the second shot.

Through his binoculars, Pablo saw the woman slump down on to the sand. It always surprised him how differently people seemed to react to the impact of a high-velocity bullet. No kill was the same.

Even before she fell, Pablo had made the call to the boat. The two brothers emerged from the brush, the third man following. Further off, the second surveillance team came out of hiding and walked towards the buggy.

The woman moved. Blood was coming from her mouth. Her hands were stretched towards the man's body by the buggy. It was as if she was trying to reach him.

Pablo looked down at the uncontrolled movements the woman was making. He'd seen it all before. Just death throes, like a beheaded chicken.

His brother went up to the man, turned him over, put the TCI between his eyes and fired. The instructions had been very clear.

He turned walked back and stood beside his brother. The other men had kept their distance.

The brothers looked down at the woman, gurgling and spitting blood. They stood there like two toreros waiting for a mortally-wounded bull to stop moving and for the corrida to end.

'Es guapa' said one of the men. She's a looker. Then he put the TCI behind Carolina's head and fired.

Half an hour later they were ready to lift the bodies into the boat and head back out to sea. They had collected up everything of a personal nature they had found in the house, including the phone and laptop, the couple's passports and clothing. Then they produced some petrol and a cigarette lighter.

They chugged out to sea, watching the house blazing. The fire brigade would never come to this part of the island, even if someone saw the fire and called them.

That afternoon the Cochabamba brothers were already on a plane to Colombia. Before taking off, Pedro had made a call from a phone booth at the airport to a number in Mexico DF. The number belonged to La Unidad and was automatically switched to a number in Colombia. Pedro Cochabamba confirmed that the contract had been carried out as per requirements, and hung up.

A few minutes later, La Unidad gave Lisker the news as he was in discussions with Rheinman in London about the financial damage he had suffered through his Virtuvio holding.

POSTSCRIPT

Later that night in New York, Mario Anfield arrived home from his European and Far East trip to find an email from his brother Paul, dated a few days earlier. Attached to the message was a very large file.

The message read:

Ciao Mario, hope you're well. Did you finally get Liverpool FC's business? I want you to be the first one to hear my news - I finally found her. Don't laugh! This is it, she is the one. She's called Carolina. I'll introduce her when I get back to New York.

Not sure when I'll be back though. I'm also writing to you about something else. You're the only one I can really trust with this. The attached is a file compiled over the years by our uncle Lenny. DON'T READ IT! Its contents are keeping me and Carolina on the run – I don't know for how long.

Mario – I know you have very good personal contacts in the world of newspapers, magazines etc. Please send the file to them, let them read it and get a professional opinion on what to do and how to publish it.

Speak soon.
Paul